Miles Davis,
Miles Smiles,
and the Invention of
Post Bop

Miles Davis,

Miles Smiles,

and the Invention of
Post Bop

JEREMY YUDKIN

INDIANA UNIVERSITY PRESS
Bloomington and Indianapolis

Miles Davis, May 3, 1960. © Bettmann/Corbis.

This book is a publication of

Indiana University Press
601 North Morton Street
Bloomington, IN 47404-3797 USA

http://iupress.indiana.edu

Telephone orders	800-842-6796
Fax orders	812-855-7931
Orders by e-mail	iuporder@indiana.edu

The paper used in this publication meets the minimum
requirements of American National Standard for
Information Sciences—Permanence of Paper for Printed
Library Materials, ANSI Z39.48-1984.

Manufactured in the United States of America

Library of Congress Cataloging-in-Publication Data

Yudkin, Jeremy.
    Miles Davis, Miles smiles, and the invention of
        post bop / Jeremy Yudkin.
        p.   cm.
    Includes bibliographical references (p.   ),
    discography (p.   ), and index.
    ISBN 978-0-253-21952-7 (pbk.)
    1. Davis, Miles.   2. Jazz musicians—United States.
    3. Davis, Miles. Miles smiles.   4. Jazz—1961-1970—History
and criticism.   5. Jazz—1961-1970—Analysis, appreciation.
    I. Title.
    ML419.D39Y83 2007
    788.9'2165092—dc22   2007015725

1   2   3   4   5   13   12   11   10   09   08

Don't write about
the music. The music
speaks for itself.

—Miles Davis, 1961

CONTENTS

For Kathryn

Acknowledgments

I am grateful to the people who have read this book in manuscript and offered their comments and suggestions. Most of them are acknowledged in the footnotes; others include my students on both sides of the Atlantic, especially Lisa Scoggin and Michael Nock, and the readers for Indiana University Press, Larry Dwyer and John Joyce, to whom I offer my sincere thanks. Trumpeter Thomas Manuel and drummer Matthew Persing were both generous with their time. A particular debt of gratitude is due to Zbigniew Granat, with whom I have discussed jazz in all its aspects for many years. For the transcriptions I had a great deal of initial aural and technical help from medievalist and rock guitarist Todd Scott and additional help from jazz pianist and master carpenter Robert Kelly, whose fine ear caught many of my errors and whose computer skills (and patience) I called upon in formulating the final versions of the musical examples. I am most grateful to Teo Macero for sharing with me his reminiscences of nearly twenty years of working closely with Miles Davis. And, as always, I thank my family for their support, especially my wife, Kathryn, for whom this slender mention is a token of my deep appreciation.

Introduction

Miles Davis was an icon of twentieth-century America—instantly recognizable both in pictures (S-shaped back, trumpet at a downward angle) and in sound (muted on trumpet, hoarse of voice). He was also an outsider. The first reason for this is that he lived in the world of jazz. Jazz musicians speak their own language, the language of flat seconds, altered chords, and tritone substitutions. And yet, of course, they also speak to nonexperts, for alongside their language is a metalanguage—the language of feelings, in which wit, melancholy, joy, anguish, pain, solitude, togetherness, frenetic intensity, and dreamy calm are expressed and received in a place beyond words. We all know this. And Miles Davis learned the secret of meaningful communication: speak only when you have something to say. His thoughtful, laconic phrasing, his careful choices of notes, the personal quality of his sound, the sense that he is constantly striving for expression—these make his conversations with us like that of no other musician in jazz.

Davis was an outsider for other reasons, too. He was black in a predominantly white culture. He was reminded of the color of his skin on many occasions. At one point, standing outside a New York club whose marquee bore his name, he was struck repeatedly on the head by a white policeman wielding a truncheon—and then charged with resisting arrest. This horrible incident is emblematic of the constant incidents of racism woven into his daily life.[1]

He was also small, and he made up for this by developing a tough exterior and by learning how to box. He was preternaturally handsome, and women black and white were strongly attracted to him. He became rich and famous, and he had to hide in his expensive house to maintain his solitude. Finally, like all people with extraordinary artistic gifts, he was an outsider because of his genius.

In the history of American jazz, Davis's contributions appear more often than those of any other musician. He was a prime mover in the cool jazz style of the late 1940s and early 1950s, he played vividly in bebop combos, and he recorded the first examples of the new hard-bop style of the mid-1950s. In 1959 he put together the sextet for the completely new modal music of *Kind of Blue,* and by the late 1960s he had invented yet another new musical genre by merging jazz and rock styles into fusion. Toward the end of his life he brought together jazz and hip-hop, jazz and funk, jazz and pop. He was the most influential and inventive jazz musician of the second half of the twentieth century. In this book I suggest that in addition to all of these achievements he must also be credited with the invention of a mid-1960s musical style that has sometimes been given the slippery title *post bop.* Previous attempts to define this term have included "vague," "the heyday of mainstream modern jazz," "mainstream jazz styles," "another term for hard bop," and, particularly unhelpfully, "post-bebop chronologically."[2]

Many of Davis's albums have been considered landmarks in the remarkable musical journey I have outlined. The tracks put together as the *Birth of the Cool* album (recorded in 1949 and 1950) are seen as harbingers of a completely new style. Everyone agrees that the 1959 *Kind of Blue* album is a classic of the genre. And the fusion movement in jazz is traced back to the remarkable *Bitches Brew* of 1969. The music of the mid-1960s, however, is usually overlooked in a review of these landmarks. It is difficult music, abstract in the extreme, and highly intense, whether fast or slow. Few attempts have been made to analyze this music or to place it in the context of Davis's life or the social ambiance of the time. Here I propose that another album should be added to the list of the most influential recordings in Davis's career: the 1967 recording *Miles Smiles.*

Davis's achievements depended on his playing, certainly, but more importantly on his ability constantly to reimagine the music, to see how jazz could move into new areas of expression. He was an orchestrator, a casting director, a pioneer. Again and again he envisioned new ways of making music, and he always put exactly the right people in place to make them happen.

The first four chapters in this book demonstrate the ways in which Davis reimagined music from 1949 to 1959—in the small-band sessions arising from his collaboration with arranger Gil Evans and in the small combos that made his mid- and late 1950s work so strong. He developed a distinctive sound, and his solo playing became thoughtful and creative, but it was his constantly new ideas and the new ways he "orchestrated" a small combo that made his recordings stand out. I illustrate this by looking closely at "Boplicity" as an example of the new cool sound, "Bags' Groove" as heralding hard bop and displaying the thoughtful mastery of Davis as a soloist, and the music of *Milestones* as the first (beautifully "orchestrated") recording of the great sextet of 1958 and 1959. One chapter is devoted to the next breakthrough—*Kind of Blue*—its musicians and its music, and I show why the album has such a special place in our imaginations. After *Kind of Blue*, in the early 1960s, Davis went into a slump. I explain the causes of this depression and lack of productivity, which are both societal and personal, but primarily musical. Chapters 7 and 8 examine the ways the Second Quintet was gradually formed and why its formation was so vital to the reinvigoration of Miles the musician. Finally in the last two chapters I focus closely on the music of *Miles Smiles*, looking at every track and explaining what is happening. I also provide musical examples of what I have to say. Most of this music has never been transcribed before, and I hope that my transcriptions (taken directly from the recordings) will be useful for those who wish to analyze the structural elements of this new style. Through these means I try to elucidate more precisely the meaning of the term *post bop*.

In the meantime I hope to establish *Miles Smiles* in the Davis canon as the pathbreaking album it is and to encourage more Davis fans and jazz scholars to listen closely to it and to the rest of the music he made during the second half of the 1960s. I think they will discover that this is not just "transitional" time that Davis spent between *Kind of Blue* and *Bitches Brew*, but a vitally creative period in the life of one of the great communicators in jazz.

Miles Davis,
Miles Smiles,
and the Invention of
Post Bop

1. Miles Smiles?

Before the release of his striking album of 1967, recorded toward the end of 1966, Miles Davis hadn't done much smiling recently.[1] He had spent much of the previous year out of action due to severe pain from his arthritic left hip and two operations to repair and ultimately replace the joint. Three months in early 1966 were lost to an inflammation of the liver.[2] He was also concentrating hard on finding his way through the turbulence of the 1960s. The imminent death of jazz was being forecast more often than usual and with more cause, and Davis was forced to react to several other phenomena of the time, both musical and social.

The most overwhelming musical maelstrom of the time was rock music. The first tour of the Beatles to the United States in 1964 began the American version of Beatlemania. This first trip lasted only nine days but was responsible for the sale of millions of records. In 1965 a multicity tour garnered completely unprecedented profits of $56 million. In today's star-weary world, it is hard to remember how startling was the phenomenon of rock in the mid-1960s. The Beatles were only one of many such supernovae in a two-year period that saw the early ascendancy of the Rolling Stones, the Who, Jefferson Airplane, the first products of the Berry Gordy Motown assembly line, and the electrification of Bob Dylan on *Bringing It All Back Home* and *Highway 61 Revisited* (both 1965) and the double album known as *Blonde on Blonde* (1966). Davis noted that "all of a sudden jazz became passé. . . . All of a sudden rock 'n' roll was in the forefront of the media."[3] The end of the decade saw Davis adopt many of the elements of rock music: electrification, synthetic instruments, heavy bass, and multiple percussion. There was also the creation of persona—the clothes, the iconoclasm, the *sprezzatura*—itself reminiscent of the aura of Dylan.[4] Then, too, Davis had to come to terms with the powerful disintegrative forces of so-called free jazz, in the two modes adopted by John Coltrane and Ornette Coleman and idiosyncratically exemplified by Charles Mingus and Eric Dolphy (often together from 1960 to 1964) and Cecil Taylor. Coleman's *Free Jazz* album of 1960 (Atlantic 1364-2) was not the first recorded example of collective improvisation, but it was certainly the most influential. Coleman's work represented an avant-garde that further divided jazz audiences and that was at first highly unattractive to Davis.

The jazz culture was disintegrating in other ways. Many of the clubs along 52nd Street in New York, the Mecca of American jazz, had been forced to close for lack of patronage or had become strip joints, and several dance halls and ballrooms had either closed down or changed to a movie format.[5] Even the famous Birdland, founded in honor of Charlie Parker in 1949, closed its doors on Broadway and 52nd in 1965, and the site was taken over for a rock club.[6]

Miles was also getting "blacker."[7] Handsome black faces graced the covers of his recordings from the 1960s, including his own and those of his wives Frances Taylor Davis and Cicely Tyson. The 1960s quintet was all black, although Davis collaborated frequently with white musicians. Most important among these were Gil Evans, of course, the arranger and composer for *Birth of the Cool* (1949 and 1950), *Miles Ahead, Porgy and Bess,* and *Sketches of Spain* (all late 1950s); [8] Bill Evans on *Kind of Blue* (1959); and Joe Zawinul, John McLaughlin, and David Holland for the fusion albums in the late 1960s. Perhaps the most enduring relationship of his life was with Teo Macero, his white record producer. Davis and Macero worked together for nearly twenty years, and Macero has referred to the relationship as a "marriage."[9] Certainly Davis stayed with Macero longer than he did with any of his wives or indeed with any other musical collaborator.

Issues of social justice and racial equality were higher than ever on the list of cultural concerns in the mid-1960s. The year 1961 had seen the beginning of the Freedom Rides and the bus boycott of Albany, Georgia. In 1963 police assaulted demonstrators in Birmingham, Alabama; Medgar Evers was murdered in Jackson, Mississippi; and Martin Luther King delivered his famous "I have a dream" speech in front of 200,000 civil rights marchers in Washington, D.C. The Civil Rights Act of 1964 was followed in 1965 by passage of the Voting Rights Act. Music was at the forefront of these concerns (as with many others of social and cultural consequence, including sexual freedom, war protest, and drugs). Witness Bob Dylan's "Oxford Town" (1963), about the resistance at the University of Mississippi to the matriculation of a black student, "The Lonesome Death of Hattie Carroll" (1964), and "A Pawn in Their Game" (1964), about the death of Medgar Evers.

In 1965 two strongly contrasted images presented themselves to the American public. While ghettos burned in Watts and Harlem, popular music and jazz reflected the "black is beautiful" emphasis of soul. James Brown ("Soul Brother Number

One"), Otis Redding ("The King of Soul"), Ray Charles ("The Genius of Soul"), and Aretha Franklin ("Lady Soul") were swept along as music drenched in blackness swelled the wave of popular music in the mid-1960s. Black themes colored the recordings of John Coltrane, not only in their religious fervor (which, though not an exclusively black theme, is a powerful element of soul) but also in the occasional wordless protest (for example, the keening "Alabama" [1963]). Both free jazz and hard bop were deeply infused with black influences—political, aesthetic, and musical. Miles Davis's black-tinged titles from the mid-1960s include "Freedom Jazz Dance," "Prince of Darkness," "Hand Jive," "Black Comedy," and "I Have a Dream."

In 1965, therefore, Davis was faced with unprecedented challenges to his sense of self and the place of his music in the contemporary world. What is remarkable is that he not only survived these challenges but overcame them to embark upon a period of extraordinarily creative productivity. Between January 1965 and June 1968, Miles Davis did many things, including tour the world and spend over a year and a half in the hospital or recuperating from a serious illness. But if for nothing else, this period will be remembered for six albums recorded by Miles Davis and his band, in which a wholly new approach to music making is attempted, extraordinary risks are taken, and performances are captured that stand among the most intense and intriguing of the genre.[10] Jack Chambers writes, "For reviewers and fans alike, [these six recordings] belong at or very near the apex of Davis's achievements as a jazz musician."[11] For Todd Coolman, the recordings document "what is arguably the greatest single transition of musical style in all of modern jazz."[12] In his book 'Round about Midnight: A Portrait of Miles Davis, Eric Nisenson states: "The albums Miles made with the 1960s quintet are among the most important work of his career."[13] Harvey Pekar describes the mid-1960s quintet as "the most unjustifiably neglected group that Miles Davis ever led."[14] And Bill Kirchner states categorically: "Today [1997], the Davis quintet of the mid-to late 1960s is revered as one of the finest ensembles in jazz history."[15] This achievement must be seen as all the more impressive given the adversity of the cultural and social context in which Davis was working.

What Davis did was to establish a family from within which he could fight these personal and artistic battles in a way that would satisfy his creative cravings. He put together a group of musicians with whom he could work, whom he could lead, and whose musical integrity and individuality were such that Davis could both mold them and learn from them at the same time. His spiky and difficult personality was turned only to the outside world. Within the group, Ron Carter said, he was "friendly and open . . . willing to lend you money or even borrow it for you, always ready to invite you to lunch or dinner. . . . I have only superlatives for the man."[16] The central element of strong family dynamics prevailed. Herbie Hancock says: "We had absolute trust in each other's ability to respond to whatever would happen. . . . You could just throw something out there just because you felt it, and you would know you could trust that something would come back."[17] Even more than in most families, there was unanimity in this group. "Collectively," says Carter, "We were a mind of one."[18] And in a 2000 interview Wayne Shorter recalled the magic and excitement of working together:

> We didn't even say anything to each other. In fact, we never even talked about anything. We never discussed what we were doing afterwards or before. But we all knew that we were going into some territory, some virgin territory or some points unknown. And you know what? Miles asked me, he said, "Do you ever get the feeling that you can play anything you want to play?" And before I answered, he said, "I know what you mean." He said [*whispering, imitating Miles*], "I know what you mean." [*laughs*] "You can play anything that you want to play." I was getting ready to answer, and he said, "I know

what you mean," and he walked away. So I walked away, too. [*laughs*] We had a good time.[19]

No wonder the band called their first studio album *E.S.P.* Looking back in his autobiography, Davis gave the band his highest accolade: "I knew right away that this was going to be a motherfucker of a group."[20]

The sextet of the late 1950s—with Cannonball Adderley, John Coltrane, Wynton Kelly (sometimes Red Garland and/or Bill Evans), Paul Chambers, and Jimmy Cobb (sometimes Philly Joe Jones)—had produced much fine music as well as one of the most enduring albums of twentieth-century jazz: *Kind of Blue*. But like Bob Dylan, Miles Davis never looked backwards. The quintet of the mid-1960s was, if anything, even more productive than the sextet of the late 1950s. And of the six albums released during those years, 1965–69, the one that most successfully balances innovation and tradition, the one whose intellectual component is sufficiently rigorous to support radical musical change and the bounding energy of five highly independent-minded individuals, is *Miles Smiles,* featuring a completely uncharacteristic eyebrows-to-chin shot of a broadly grinning Davis on a background of hot orange. On the six tracks of this album, recorded without alternate takes on two consecutive days in October 1966, the intense seriousness of the participants is patently obvious. The fire and energy of these performances cauterize every blemish (there are several) and overshadow some ragged uncertainties of ensemble and direction, whose combined effect, far from detracting from the spirit of the music, lend it the immediacy and dangerousness of a high-wire act. The six performances (again, these were all first takes) of *Miles Smiles* are "Circle," "Orbits," "Dolores," "Freedom Jazz Dance," "Ginger Bread Boy," and "Footprints." They were recorded in this order, the first four on October 24, the last two on October 25, 1966. On the album itself, the order of the first two is reversed, and "Footprints" is placed third, putting

"Orbits," "Circle," and "Footprints" on the first side of the LP and "Dolores," "Freedom Jazz Dance," and "Ginger Bread Boy" (alternately "Gingerbread Boy") on the second.[21]

Almost everything is fresh in these six performances. Most notable are the adoption of a kind of elastic form that can stretch to accommodate creative improvisation;[22] employment of uncommon time signatures and reinterpretation of familiar ones; reconceived roles for drums and bass; redefinition of the piano as a horn; full engagement in both the precompositional and the performance-compositional modes by both horn players; a flatter, more floating, and rhythmically more varied approach to the creation of solo lines; melodic as well as harmonic reminiscence; a multifaceted juxtaposition of momentum and stasis; a reversal of the locus of greater activity from soloists to drummer; and the replacement of much of the responsibility for timekeeping from drums to bass, thus freeing the drummer in the direction of unprecedented flexibility. These are the specific elements that make up the new style that we can call post bop. Analysis of *Miles Smiles* also permits us to make direct comparison of three of the tracks ("Footprints," "Freedom Jazz Dance," and "Ginger Bread Boy") with recordings of the "same" material from within the previous couple of years, thus showing dramatically what is new in the post-bop style.

But before we can understand the historic breakthrough of *Miles Smiles* and the significance of its position in Miles Davis's output, we need to look back at his musical accomplishments in the years leading up to the formation of the second great quintet. What we shall discover is a career with a slow beginning, a meteoric ascent, and a disconcerting collapse before the revivifying period of the mid-1960s.

2. Birth

Davis's style was established over the years from 1949 to 1959. He had apprenticed with Charlie Parker since the mid-1940s, and it was perhaps in sheer self-defense that he developed his epigrammatic way of playing and his tendency to use the lower register of his instrument. Against Parker's flurry of notes and Dizzy Gillespie's high-energy, high-stratosphere playing, Davis's style is clearly differentiated.

His first important work was in the context of the nonet that was gathered together to make the recordings that ultimately came to be known as *The Birth of the Cool*. This title was only retrospectively applied to the highly influential small-big-band sessions recorded in January and April 1949 and March 1950.[1] Remarkably for a young man of twenty-three, Davis had a contract for twelve sides from Capitol Records, and under the guidance of Gil Evans he brought together an unusual combination of players.[2] The nonet of *Birth of the Cool* fame stood halfway be-

tween the normal bop quintet and the big band of twelve to sixteen pieces. It featured trumpet, alto sax, and a rhythm section
(piano, bass, drums), like a bop combo, but it also included four
other instruments, two of which were conventional for a big
band and two of which were not. Davis and Evans had in mind
a special smoother sound, so in addition to the normal trombone
and baritone sax they used a French horn and a tuba. The result
was a mellow, mid- to low-range sound, capable of flexibility
and rhythmic subtlety. Max Harrison has described the sound
of the band as one in which "the sounds of all the instruments
were fused in a texture whose parts moved with a supple fluidity that contrasted with the hard, bright, darting lines of bop."[3]
The main soloists, apart from Davis, included the alto saxophonist Lee Konitz, baritone saxophonist Gerry Mulligan, and
pianist John Lewis. It was early in their careers for all of these
men, and they shared a common characteristic: a light, smooth
style of playing, evenly rhythmic with subtle swing, that stood
in contrast to the unpredictability and irregular bursts of bop.
Konitz and Mulligan were twenty-two; John Lewis was twenty-
nine. At thirty-seven Gil Evans was the gray eminence behind
the group. He had made a name for himself as an arranger for
the Claude Thornhill Orchestra, where he favored a smooth texture, rich in medium and low brass and light on the vibrato.[4] The
relationship between Evans and Davis was based on mutual re-
spect. "He liked the way I played, and I liked the way he wrote,"
Davis said. As Evans put it, "We had this thing—this sound—in
common."[5]

Evans lived in a small basement apartment in New York,
which served as a kind of informal meeting house in which jazz
musicians gathered and talked.[6] As Mulligan recalled, "Everybody seemed to gravitate to Gil's place."[7] These were knowl-
edgeable men. Apart from the immense amount of knowledge
they picked up by playing, many of them had formal training.[8]

Davis had come to New York from East St. Louis to attend Juilliard (although his attendance there was brief and spotty). Konitz had studied with a member of the Chicago Symphony Orchestra as well as with Lennie Tristano. Mulligan played many reed instruments and had learned the piano; he was also a composer and arranger who worked for Gene Krupa's big band and contributed scores to the Thornhill Orchestra. John Lewis studied music at the University of New Mexico and earned a master's degree from the Manhattan School of Music; he also spent time in Europe, studying piano and composing.[9]

The personnel also reflected a melding of big-band and bop backgrounds. Both saxophonists, the French horn player, the tuba player, and the bassist on the first recording session came from the Thornhill Orchestra. Davis, Lewis, and Max Roach, the drummer, were active in current bop groups. The trombone player, Kai Winding, had backgrounds in both camps. (Personnel changed slightly from session to session.) Two other factors may have played a role in the size of the group. No band of any size could ignore the originality and fecundity of Ellington, and some of Ellington's early recordings had used a relatively small group. Ellington's 1927 recording of "East St. Louis Toddle-Oo" was colorful, transparent, fairly slow, and used only ten players. The second factor was simply economics: the fewer players there were in a new band, the more likely it was that they would get hired.[10] As Davis said in his autobiography, a club owner would balk even at nine people. "[He didn't want] to be paying nine motherfuckers when he could have paid five."[11] Despite all the work on the arrangements and all the rehearsal, in the end the group was booked (at the Royal Roost on Broadway) for only two weeks.[12]

Twelve tracks were recorded in the three recording sessions. Although the stamp of Gil Evans is clearly on all the pieces, the product was really a joint effort. It was Davis's first job as leader. "He took the initiative and put the theories to work," Mulligan reported many years later. "He called the rehearsals, hired the halls, called the players, and generally cracked the whip."[13] Mulligan himself is responsible for five of the tracks, the originals "Venus de Milo," "Rocker," and "Jeru" (his own nickname) and the arrangements "Godchild" and "Darn That Dream." Lewis contributed his own "Rouge" and arranged "Move" and "Budo." Davis wrote "Deception," and Evans contributed his own original "Moon Dreams" and arranged his and Davis's "Boplicity." The only piece from outside the circle is by composer, trumpeter, and arranger Johnny Carisi, whose sophisticated blues "Israel" was written while he was studying with classical composer Stefan Wolpe.[14] What was common to the whole enterprise was Davis's vision and artistic oversight. Mulligan made this very clear: "Miles dominated that band completely; the whole nature of the interpretation was his."[15]

All of the tracks, each of which had to fit on one side of a 78-rpm record, are short, ranging from two and a quarter to three and a half minutes. The effect on the music is considerable: solos are brief, no more than a single chorus and often less, allowing no room for lengthy trajectory or the building of complex structures, and attention therefore falls more strongly on the composed areas of each piece. Even during solos, there is considerable interaction between soloist and the group and a more integrated relationship between them. Note, for example, how Mulligan floats to the top in occasional phrases of full-chorus statements in "Jeru." The group choruses are beautifully rehearsed, managing to convey smooth affect and clean counterpoint with no loss of spontaneity. The texture is clear and transparent with melody often doubled (trumpet with alto sax) over a strong low range (reinforced by baritone sax and tuba). Sometimes the balance is reversed. On Mulligan's arrangement of "Godchild," the lead is taken by baritone sax and tuba playing in unison, answered by the higher instruments. Davis is restrained, open-horn, midrange, hardly ever double-timing. His solos are thoughtful and original if not inspired, leaning on bop phrases and clichés, such as the triplet turn, although he runs phrases against and across formal patterns such as the eight-bar units of the AABA structure and is starting to learn the expressivity of silent moments. Both saxophone players play straight tone with little vibrato: Konitz on alto is fleet and light, Mulligan amazingly flexible on the normally unwieldy or gruff baritone. They can be heard juxtaposed on "Rocker." Lewis has a delicious quiet eight bars in "Boplicity" and another sixteen on his own "Rouge." The final track recorded is a discreet arrangement of the slow ballad "Darn That Dream" with singer Kenny Hagood. With the singer in the foreground most of the time, there is not much room for the band to shine, although Miles slips in a couple of elegant fills between sections and takes a simple paraphrase-solo on a penultimate eight-measure A section.

Tempos are slower than usual at that time. In contrast to bop, where tempos run from fast to blazing, most of the selections are medium tempo; "Boplicity" is comfortable, "Darn That Dream" slow, and "Moon Dreams" glacial. Forms are mostly based on the thirty-two-bar AABA pattern, but there is some manipulation of section length: for example, by extending the second bridge (B) on "Boplicity" to ten measures and the A sections in "Deception" to fourteen. On this last piece it is hard to hear where the sections begin and end. The harmonic writing in "Deception," true to its name, is also deliberately misleading. Rather than starting each section with the home key, as is normal, Davis opens them with an unstable chord that suggests "middle" rather than "beginning." He also disguises the opening of the piece with a half-statement of the A section, in other words, a phrase of seven measures, so that we are misled from the outset. Further, a phrase toward the end of the section sounds, both melodically and harmonically, like a beginning.[16] Davis borrows and reworks here a composition by George Shearing entitled "Conception." Davis liked to play games with titles as well as with music. The original is already a sophisticated piece. In 1949, Shearing was just beginning to popularize his own very distinctive "cool" sound, with the piano melody doubled by (unvibrating) vibraphone and (an octave lower) by piano left hand and guitar.[17] Davis's reworking of Shearing's piece is the first of several compositions in which he pays tribute to another composer while demonstrating that his own edits are an improvement on the original.

The most significant performance of the twelve is "Boplicity," recorded at the second session on April 22, 1949. This piece is a supreme instance of the sophisticated arranging skill of Gil Evans, the polished but subtly swinging style of the band, the smooth surface and underlying complexity of cool, and the birth of the individuality of Miles Davis. It is a performance of just under three minutes (2'59" on the clock), and it can be enjoyed in many ways, for its smooth sound, laid-back style, and relaxed tempo (68 beats to the minute) hide some fascinating complexities. On the surface, "Boplicity" is a straightforward 32-bar AABA form in three choruses. Soloists are Gerry Mulligan (baritone sax), Davis (trumpet), and John Lewis (piano) in that order. The piece starts out clearly with the whole ensemble playing the first chorus. The sound is smooth, horns playing parallel lines over a relaxed walking bass, and drums are light—mostly brushes on cymbals—and in the background. The second A has a slight rhythmic variation in the second measure, but this is clearly composed and piquing rather than disruptive. The divisions between sections are clearly signaled, with a long held note at the end of each A. The B section has a change of melody and harmony, moving away from the home key and then back to it, but the sense of stability is retained by the continuing smooth ensemble texture and the unruffled rhythm. Mulligan solos on the first two As of the second chorus. His sound is light but intimate, the outline gentle, the rhythm carefree and swinging. He is accompanied only by the rhythm section, bass still walking, drums still light, piano comping discreetly. The band comes back in on the bridge of this second chorus, and here things change. The listener will be forgiven for getting slightly, though intriguingly, lost. The first four measures of the bridge are extended to six, ending on a rich low sonority with baritone and bass. The texture here is lighter, as we notice that the trumpet is missing. To tell the truth, we notice this only in retrospect, on the next four measures of the bridge, because here Davis starts to solo, with warm golden tone—midrange—and lovely phrasing. The sound is a treat, enhanced by its absence earlier among the fluty sounds of the reeds. The band comes back in for the last A section of this chorus with Davis still prominent at the top of the sound. This A section has been recomposed, but its function as a closer to the chorus is clear, and we are reassured as to our location in the form. Davis now takes the first two As of the third and final chorus, but this time, with great subtlety, the band floats in and out of the texture, now providing light punctuation to statements, now settling back in to accompany the trumpet. Davis devises some very pretty melodic lines, with unusual phrasing, a creative use of variable rhythm, and, paradoxically, an intensification of the expression by means of significant and unexpectedly placed silences (see Example 1). John Lewis solos over the bridge in a very clever, spare, jaunty little eight-bar, right-hand-only solo, accompanied just by drums and bass. This is the lightest texture in the piece. The whole performance is rounded off by a return to the A section as played at the beginning, with the last measure drawn out.

As with the playing, the simple exterior of the harmony disguises considerable richness. The piece is in F, and the bridge moves to the subdominant (B♭) and then the dominant (C7), as is conventional, but along the way there are some unusual harmonic colors. Each of the A sections, for example, begins in G minor, and the bridge moves to E♭ (actually a more delicious E♭7#5) and then A7 by means of B♭ minor and B minor (a half-step away) before going to its proper place. The sonorities are richer

Example 1. Miles Davis solo on "Boplicity" from *Birth of the Cool* (1950), starting at bridge of second chorus.

than is common, depending on ninth, eleventh, and thirteenth chords. Much of the ensemble work is in five- or six-part harmony. The parallel lines of the horns and the generally quiet dynamics also innocently disguise some spicy chords, with unexpected sharps and flats. The texture is also constantly shifting, as though the individual instruments were threads in a complex fabric interwoven in changing combinations. This effect is enhanced by the fact that there is only one of each instrument in the ensemble.

These three minutes are spectacular. In 1950 Davis named "Boplicity" as the favorite among his recordings. It has been called a "tour de force," "brilliant," "enough to make Gil Evans qualify as one of jazz's greatest arranger-composers," and "an incontestable masterpiece."[18] Together with the other recordings of the nonet, it also marked the beginning of a decade of extraordinary growth and accomplishment for Miles Davis.

Many of the people involved in the project regarded it as formative. Gerry Mulligan later said, "I consider myself fortunate to be there, and I thank whatever lucky stars [were] responsible for placing me there. There's a kind of perfection about those recordings." It was the birth of something important for many of the participants. It was also a birth for Miles Davis—as an original player and a highly original thinker.

3. Groove

Miles Davis's career had started out propitiously. He had come to attention in New York playing with Charlie Parker and had put together the famous nonet for the influential *Birth of the Cool* sessions. But it wasn't until 1954 that he began to realize the promise of 1949. And the most compelling example of that realization came with his recording of a Milt Jackson blues, "Bags' Groove," at the very end of 1954.

The recording session that produced "Bags' Groove" took place on December 24, 1954, a little more than five and a half years after the "Boplicity" recording from *Birth of the Cool*. The recording engineer was the legendary Rudy Van Gelder, who five years earlier had begun recording as a hobby in the living room of his parents' house in Hackensack, New Jersey. Although, like many influential figures in the history of jazz, Van Gelder had another profession (optometrist), he became the principal recording engineer for Blue Note in 1953 and made recordings for Prestige and Savoy starting in 1954. It wasn't until

1959 that he had his own studio and worked full-time in music.[1] His recordings of the bebop and hard-bop groups of the 1950s and early 1960s are among the classics of jazz, and the clarity and balance of his sound, recorded in the years before multichannel recording devices were invented, remain unmatched.[2] Davis had recorded for Prestige in 1951 and again in 1953, with some sessions for Blue Note in 1952. In 1954 he recorded one session for Blue Note, but all the rest in that year were for Prestige.

The years between *Birth of the Cool* and the end of 1954 had been problematic for Davis. Soon after the 1949 session that produced "Boplicity," Davis became addicted to heroin. Considering that he had been with Charlie Parker since he first came to New York in 1945, it is remarkable that he resisted temptation for as long as he did. In September 1950 Davis was arrested in Los Angeles for possession of narcotics, a fact given considerable publicity by *Down Beat* in November.[3] His reputation suffered, and it was hard for him to get jobs. He stayed addicted for three more years, playing sporadically, sometimes very poorly, and moving around the country. He did anything for money, including pimping and stealing from his friends. Biographer Jack Chambers writes that during those years "his addiction to heroin dominated his life." Davis himself said, "That's all I lived for."[4] His stature fell rapidly among producers, club owners, other musicians, and the public. He was ranked ninth in a *Down Beat* list of top trumpeters, and a distinguished jazz critic spoke of his work in the past tense. Davis described himself during those years as "sinking faster than a motherfucker towards death." Finally, probably just in time, and with characteristic self-discipline, Davis cured himself, at least for the time being, by locking himself in a room for two weeks at his father's house in East Saint Louis and sweating it out cold turkey.[5]

Miles Davis returned to New York in 1954, clean of heroin, ng physically fit through boxing and playing better than ever. "Nineteen fifty-four was a great year for me," he says in his autobiography. "A couple of the albums that were released that year . . . made everybody—the musicians—sit up and notice me again, more than ever before."[6] Also, the first LP version of the 1949/50 nonet sessions was released in that year. It was a ten-inch LP (without "Boplicity" and three other tracks), but it reminded listeners and critics of Miles in top form.

Prestige had signed Davis to a three-year recording contract, and all of the recording sessions in 1954 were for Prestige.[7] Many of the results are deservedly famous. They include "Walkin'," "Blue 'n' Boogie," "Oleo," "The Man I Love," and the phenomenal "Bags' Groove." At this time Davis had found his way to the perfect context in which to play his best. Perhaps not coincidentally it was the context in which he had first appeared before the public on arriving in New York nine years earlier and the kind of group Charlie Parker had formed with him officially in 1947: that is, a combination of players that includes at least two soloists. Miles was aware that he did not have the fluency or loquaciousness of Parker or Dizzy and that he needed a foil for his understated and oblique playing style. From 1954 until 1965 the story of Davis's career is that of his finding (and losing) people to fill that special position in his bands. "Walkin'" and "Blue 'n' Boogie" feature Lucky Thompson on tenor saxophone and J. J. Johnson on trombone in addition to Davis, in a sextet session recorded at the end of April. The June quintet session has Sonny Rollins as Davis's foil, and the quintet session from the end of December puts Milt Jackson in the role of the second soloist. It should, of course, also be noted that Davis was equally particular about his rhythm section, and in 1954 he had found three people who worked beautifully together: Horace Silver on piano, Percy Heath on bass, and Kenny Clarke on drums, the latter two appearing together frequently as two-fourths of the Modern Jazz Quartet. This unit recorded for Davis in the April and June sessions; for the December session that produced "Bags' Groove,"

Davis invited Thelonious Monk to take the pianist's bench, with famous consequences.

Miles Davis played down the incident in his autobiography, but apparently there was considerable friction between Miles and Monk at the session. Davis told Monk not to play when he was soloing. For one thing he didn't like the way that Monk played accompaniment, and for another he wanted to hear "more space in the music."[8]

Monk took exception to this kind of banishment, and tapes of some of the verbal skirmishes have survived. But some remarkable music was made that day, and some of it is a result of the creative tension in the air. For example, Davis decided to include "Bemsha Swing"—a Monk composition—on the record, perhaps as a peace offering to the pianist. Monk *does* comp behind Davis on this piece, and Davis throws in some very Monkish phrases at the end of his solo, which Monk then refers to and toys with in his solo. "I *know* Monk loved me, and I loved him, too," said Davis.[9]

Davis was still young to be leading his own group. In 1954 he was only twenty-eight. Monk, at thirty-seven, was much older and more experienced. He had played in the Coleman Hawkins Quartet and the Dizzy Gillespie big band. Between 1947 and 1952 he had made several recordings for Blue Note, in which some of his remarkable and completely original compositions had started to appear. He also appeared regularly at such important clubs as Minton's Playhouse, the Royal Roost, and the Village Vanguard. In 1952 Monk was signed to a three-year recording contract of his own with Prestige, for whom he made a record with Sonny Rollins and laid down more of his own compositions.[10] Monk was a brilliant and idiosyncratic player. His timing was impeccable; he produced harmony that was spicy and crisp, often utilizing dissonant seconds, sevenths, or tritone intervals; his runs featured essionistic and characteristic whole-tone scales; and he often ovised with short melodic nuggets that he twisted and turned into new shapes or placed at shifting points in the bar. No other pianist played like Thelonious Monk.

The second soloist at this session was Milt Jackson, a third member of the Modern Jazz Quartet, which had been formed two years earlier. He was three years older than Davis and had played with Gillespie, Parker, Monk, and Tadd Dameron. He was a member of Woody Herman's big band and small combos in 1949 and 1950, Gillespie's sextet from 1950 to 1952, and the Modern Jazz Quartet from 1952 on. Jackson's sound was also immediately identifiable. He adjusted his vibraphone to a much slower vibrato than earlier players, so that his sound was warm and natural.[11] His slow playing was soulful and intimate, and in medium or faster tempos he could vary his phrasing with amazing creativity, now spinning long lines, now producing a fiery, blues-drenched flurry of notes, whose intensity was in intimate tension with the "cool" sound of his instrument.

Percy Heath was the same age as Milt Jackson and was in wide demand as a bassist in and around New York, both for recording dates and for live gigs. He had played with Jackson since 1951, and with John Lewis and Kenny Clarke he was one of the founding members of the Modern Jazz Quartet in 1952. His playing was rock solid and yet fluent, with both rhythmic and melodic trajectory.[12] Davis had started playing with him in April 1954.

Kenny Clarke was, at forty, the oldest and most experienced member of the combo. He had played professionally since he was fifteen, and since the 1940s he had recorded with Sidney Bechet, Mildred Bailey, and Billie Holiday and had toured with Louis Armstrong and Ella Fitzgerald. During that time he also played as the house drummer at the Apollo Theater in Harlem and led the house band at Minton's Playhouse, where many of the important early bebop experiments were made. Kenny Clarke had been the drummer at the second *Birth of the Cool* session, when "Boplicity" was recorded. By 1954 he had played on about one hundred recordings. He was with the Modern Jazz Quartet until 1955, when he moved permanently to France. Clarke's playing was thoughtful, sensitive to context, and creative; he was especially known for his beautiful brush work. Davis started using him in April 1954 because, he said, "When it came to playing soft brush strokes on the drums, nobody could do it better than Klook [Clarke's nickname]."[13]

The combo for this recording session, therefore, was handpicked and expert. Each man had considerable performing and recording experience and had already formed his own style. Davis used each musician in a creative way to complement his own playing and sculpt the sound of the ensemble. Once again we must note Davis's powerful skill at choosing partners and directing them to creative ends. Indeed, in this recording it may be said that his ability to "orchestrate" the group was at least as important in the lasting quality of the music as his own playing, although his own playing reaches unprecedented heights of structure, coherence, and expression.

"Bags' Groove" was written by Milt Jackson, whose nickname was "Bags." It is a relaxed twelve-bar blues with a repeated riff as melody. The riff is a three-bar phrase, leaving the fourth empty, as is traditional for the blues. The riff is simply repeated for the second and third lines of the blues. The head is made up of two choruses, with the trumpet a third lower on the second chorus. In the first chorus Jackson plays parallel thirds below the trumpet; in the second, he plays a sixth above. The groove is laid-back, as the drums and especially the bass emphasize only two beats in the bar, thus suggesting a half-time tempo.

What comes next is perhaps one of the greatest solos in bop history. In his autobiography Davis said that at the beginning of 1954 he had decided to play bebop but "take the music forward into a more funky kind of blues."[14] There could be no better description of this performance, which is bop-styled in its laying out of the head, its succession of improvised solos, and its return to the head, but is definitely "more funky." The tempo (at about 148 beats per minute) is swinging but relaxed, easygoing but with forward motion. Both the tune and the harmony are simple but with a couple of unexpected features. These provide a wealth of possibilities for a creative improviser.

Miles takes nine choruses for his first solo. This is made possible by an important shift in recording parameters for the early 1950s: microgroove or LP recording. This allowed a recorded performance to be more of a live event, more like what musicians actually played in clubs, than the severely restricted three-minute limit of one side of a 78-rpm ten-inch record. A ten-inch LP could store fifteen minutes of music on a side, a twelve-inch LP more than twenty minutes. This track of "Bags' Groove" lasts a little over eleven minutes, a length inconceivable only a few years earlier.[15] The solo is beautifully gauged over its nine choruses (see Example 2). Miles develops slightly different musical gestures for each chorus, but to prevent too stiff a reading of the form he also often runs fluently across the "joins" between one twelve-measure chorus and the next. There is both a sense of organic unity for the entire solo and a sense of growth and increasing intensity as it progresses.[16] The last chorus reaches the highest notes and stays high in the range before descending two octaves to reclaim a relaxed middle register, touch on a gesture familiar from an earlier chorus, and bring in the vibraphone. Throughout the solo, Davis's tone is warm and relaxed, imparting a lively sense of swing through staccato notes on the offbeat. As was becoming characteristic of his style, he stays mostly in the middle register and uses silence eloquently. Breaks in the melodic flow create intriguing patterns of phrase length. Occasional fluffed notes add to rather than subtract from the sense of spontaneous creativity. Overall the effect is one of superb control and an apparently limitless supply of invention.

24   Groove

Example 2. Miles Davis solo on "Bags' Groove" take 1 from *Bags' Groove* (1954).

This solo has drawn the attention of many writers. Comments include the following:

> Davis's solo . . . [has] an oblique relentlessness and [is] full of neat, perfectly executed variations.

> Miles' beautifully logical solo . . .

> From the point of view of sound, of sheer tonal beauty, his two solos eclipse all his earlier work. . . . [They] are notable for his apparently inexhaustible supply of ideas, which seem to grow organically out of each other.

> "Bags' Groove" (take 1) is a classic, containing one of Davis's best recorded solos of the period.

> Miles's solo is near perfect—a beautiful, unfolding set of memorable ideas, each a springboard for the next. His sound . . . has a real vocal-like quality of expression. His interpretation of the blues here is deeply convincing . . .

> [This track] is surely one of the greatest jazz recordings.[17]

Jackson follows with nine choruses of his own, nicely swinging though perhaps not quite as original, and, as if to show how beautifully and subtly he can comp, Monk plays delicately behind him (after a delay of some three measures: one can almost see Davis encouraging him to play). The striking contrast in timbre alone justifies Davis's decision to have him lay out earlier. When Monk enters for his own solo, it is with a completely new sound again. He places a little gesture against the blues template in ever-varied positions like a pointillist painter. His entire solo is brilliant, flicking little phrases about, nagging the rhythm, throwing in fleeting references to his own compositions, and piquing the ear with dissonant pokes at the keyboard. Monk also gauges the trajectory of his solo over nine choruses, building gradually up to more sustained solo lines, then to chords, then to thick two-handed clusters, but (in contrast to the

Davis solo, which built up to a kind of climax) winding down again to the single lines and the piquant two-note jabs. When asked the secret of his style, Monk answered with typical brevity: "How to use notes differently. That's it. Just how to use notes differently."[18]

At the end of Monk's solo Davis comes in again as though to play the closing head, but Jackson is not there to play it with him, and Davis switches immediately to another short solo. It takes him a few seconds to gather his thoughts, however, and there is a measure or two of misdirection. Davis takes three choruses before bringing in Jackson for the close. Throughout the take, Heath keeps up a rock-steady but ambling walk, and Clarke lilts along on brushes, with the subtlest signals at the ends of choruses (and even occasionally at the end of four-measure groups) to keep everyone in line.

Amazingly the second take of "Bags' Groove" recorded at the same session is almost as good as the first. There seems to be some saliva in Davis's horn at the beginning that is only briefly distracting in another fine solo, a little more melodically flowing than the first and perhaps not quite as unified. Jackson's solo is more intense than that on the first take, with Monk noticeably more prominent behind him. Perhaps he took courage from the first take. (It also sounds as though Van Gelder has moved the mike a little closer to the drums and piano.) Jackson quits after five choruses (he took nine in the first take), leaving Monk still comping and not quite ready to solo. It takes him four measures to get going. Monk's solo is far less oblique, thicker and more garrulous, with much more two-handed playing—a completely different solo but also intriguing and wonderfully cognizant of rhythmic play. He too plays for a shorter time than in the first take: seven choruses instead of nine. Clarke taps out a clear signal on the last two measures: either he is encouraging Monk to close or he is giving Davis a warning. When Miles comes back in, he has removed the spit from his horn. After two choruses he again tries to bring Jackson in for the ending, but fails. It remains for him to complete one more chorus to precede the close, and he covers the miscue by pretending he had meant to play the head tune all along. All this is perfectly audible. This second take, played at almost exactly the same tempo as the first, is (at nine and a half minutes) about two minutes shorter overall because of both Jackson's and Monk's reduced solo time.

The creative leadership and newly invigorated playing of Miles Davis in 1954 influenced many other players in the mid-1950s. Performances like those on "Walkin' " and "Bags' Groove" also ushered in a new direction for jazz. The fast tempos and jagged lines of bebop had provided inspiration to countless players since the early 1940s, but it was time for a change. Davis's nonet sessions at the turn of the decade had already suggested one way of renewing the music: the cool style, with laid-back tempos, a more "arranged" feel, and the lower-intensity sounds of players such as Chet Baker, Paul Desmond, and Gerry Mulligan. Here Davis again rethinks musical style with his "more funky kind of blues." This style was to reach its apogee in the second half of the 1950s and the early 1960s under the name *hard bop*. Landmark recordings in the style were Horace Silver's "The Preacher" (1955) and "Moanin' " by Bobby Timmons (1958). It is perhaps indicative of the powerful influence that Miles Davis had upon those around him and especially on the man who was his pianist for five out of six of his recording sessions in 1954 that Horace Silver's "The Preacher" was recorded (by Rudy Van Gelder in the same living room in New Jersey) on February 6, 1955, about six weeks after "Bags' Groove" was made.

"Walkin' " and "Bag's Groove" certainly display the qualities that later came to be identified with hard bop: simple, repetitive, bluesy melodies, medium tempos, an earthy sound reinforced by occasional short grace notes, two-in-a-bar feel and parallel harmonies for the head, and an easy swing for the solos. I would suggest that among all his other achievements Davis should be recognized as the real progenitor of hard bop in the mid-1950s.[19] This would add one more to the list of significant changes of direction for jazz instigated by Davis himself. I note once again that he wrought these changes not only by means of his own playing but also through his own powerful musical imagination and the ways in which he selected, organized, and challenged the other players around him.

4. Voice

Charlie Parker's death in March 1955 hit Miles Davis (and everybody else in the jazz world) hard. After a pathetically brief ten-year career that flared, arced, and then sputtered out like a firework, the most brilliant improviser in the history of the music had finally succumbed to drug and alcohol abuse at the age of thirty-five.[1] Perhaps because Miles Davis had been Parker's sideman or because he represented something new, the mantle passed to Davis.

His appearance at the new jazz festival in Newport, Rhode Island, in the summer of 1955 caught everyone's attention. Davis played muted trumpet on " 'Round Midnight," and the new sound was suddenly the talk of the jazz world. A year earlier Davis had discovered the remarkable effect of playing with a Harmon mute (without the central stem) on his trumpet, placed very close to a microphone. Jazz trumpeter and Davis biographer Ian Carr explains the effect:

[The] resulting sound is full and breathy in the lower register and thin and piercing in the upper. . . . The Harmon mute can be used to express the most delicate nuances of feeling, and because its timbre is round and full and has a clear tongued edge, it is rhythmically very eloquent. With such qualities— the mixture of sweet and sour tonality and the muscularity of rhythms—it was the perfect vehicle for Miles's requirements.[2]

It also became one of the best known sounds in jazz. The editor of *Metronome* described the Newport event and the reaction. "On this night . . . Miles was superb, brilliantly absorbing. . . . [W]hatever Miles did . . . was dramatic enough to include Miles in all the columns written about the Festival."[3] From this point on, Davis's career was in the ascendance. Prestige made sure to begin a steady series of record releases, but Davis was being courted by Columbia, a company with far more clout than Prestige, more resources, and an eagerness to build up its jazz catalogue.[4] For the rest of 1955 Davis concentrated on putting together a working quintet for club dates. The rhythm section came together quickly: Red Garland (piano), Paul Chambers (bass), and Philly Joe Jones (drums). Garland was mild, straightforward, and solid, but with a light touch and transparent voicings; Chambers was a brilliant but conservative bassist, who could "walk" for miles but had an excellent ear that supported the occasional outing on bow; and Jones was a precision timepiece with subtlety and drive.[5] Although each was a fine soloist, none outshone the other, and their strength lay in their cohesiveness and their ability to generate an irresistible sense of swing behind any player. Garland and Jones were veterans at thirty-two; Chambers was a youngster at twenty and a Davis discovery. ("When I heard him I *knew* he was a bad motherfucker.")[6] Although Davis had done some playing (and recording) in the quartet format, he was still looking for a second soloist. He wanted Sonny Rollins but couldn't get him.[7] He had to make do with his second choice, a player of his own age (twenty-nine): a tenor saxophonist named John Coltrane.

Davis still owed Prestige some work, which he fulfilled in 1956, while starting work for Columbia. The group became more and more cohesive in their playing and personally close off-stage. Coltrane even had the whole band stand as best men when he married his first wife.[8] In 1956 Davis did permanent damage to his larynx by shouting too soon after a throat operation. This gained him the hoarse whisper that became his life-long trademark and, curiously, matched the sound of his muted playing. Outstanding performances include Dave Brubeck's lovely ballad "In Your Own Sweet Way"; Rodgers and Hart's "It Never Entered My Mind," with Garland playing a rippling piano accompaniment that is more classical than jazz; "If I Were a Bell," from Frank Loesser's Broadway show *Guys and Dolls;* and "My Funny Valentine," Rodgers and Hart's minor-key ballad, which Davis recorded many times and played in concerts. These, together with many other tunes, all came out on the "apostrophe" records that represented Davis's last fling with Prestige: *Workin', Steamin', Relaxin',* and *Cookin'.*[9]

At the same time, Davis made his first album for Columbia, *'Round about Midnight.* As though announcing his new commitment, Davis lays down a striking performance of the Monk tune " 'Round Midnight," which had captured the critics' attention at Newport. Davis plays with what was becoming his signature sound, on muted trumpet, with simple accompanying lines from Coltrane. The arrangement (by Gil Evans) features a cyclic form that foreshadows the symmetrical approach that is also a strong feature of *Kind of Blue.* After a sustained introduction Davis plays the tune in his original oblique manner over quiet long tones from Coltrane and then solos with some elegantly propulsive work by Chambers on bass. (On this tune Davis utilizes his technique of leaving out the final, resolving note of a melody—on

"In Your Own Sweet Way" he had deliberately played a wrong one—a device that moves the music forward rather than sectioning it off.) Outbursts from the band and a drum roll introduce a middle section that moves into double time, marked by a strongly swinging rhythm section over which Coltrane plays his simultaneously ebullient and thoughtful solo. A sudden stop and Davis brings the music back to the tempo and hushed sound of the opening.

Already the rhythm section has learned how to differentiate among the solo players. On this and the other tunes on the album, the players leave plenty of space for Davis, drive the pulse behind Coltrane, and provide a comfortable, easy swing for Garland.

At first Davis dealt with the marked contrast between his tense, restrained approach and Coltrane's extroverted loquacity by leaving Coltrane off the ballads. But " 'Round Midnight" shows that Davis had now learned to use the contrast for musical advantage, an advantage he exploits in all their later recordings. The involvement of Gil Evans, Davis's friend and collaborator on the *Birth of the Cool* sessions, as the arranger of this famous track (although he wasn't given credit for it until nearly twenty years later) began a new series of collaborations between the two men.[10]

Unfortunately, every one of Davis's sidemen at this time suffered from heroin addiction. The unreliability that this produced resulted in several firings and rehirings, with Coltrane being replaced by Rollins for six months, Garland by Tommy Flanagan for two, and Jones by Art Taylor for six, all in 1957. It also probably contributed to tragically early deaths for two of them. Coltrane died at the age of forty and Chambers at thirty-three.

Davis now began work on another project with Gil Evans. Columbia sponsored a recording of a big band with nineteen musicians and Davis as soloist playing Evans's arrangements of all kinds of tunes, ranging from jazz standards to a pop song to classical or semiclassical numbers. In the former group are "Springsville" by Johnny Carisi, one of the composers featured on *Birth of the Cool* (who also played trumpet in this band), Dave Brubeck's "The Duke," Davis and Evans's "Miles Ahead," Evans's "Blues for Pablo," Ahmad Jamal's "New Rhumba," Bobby Troup's "The Meaning of the Blues" (he was also the composer of "Route 66"), and J. J. Johnson's "Lament." The pop song is the last track on the album: "I Don't Wanna Be Kissed (by Anyone Else but You)." The classical pieces are "The Maids of Cadiz" by the nineteenth-century French composer Léo Delibes, which marks the beginning of Evans and Davis's attraction to music with a Spanish flavor, and Kurt Weill's "My Ship" from *Lady in the Dark.*

This is a highly varied program (entitled *Miles Ahead* by Columbia),[11] but the album is tied together by the elegant orchestral arrangements and the burnished sound of Davis on flugelhorn, which sounds mellow even when high and restrained even when loud. The unity provided by these two elements, which share the qualities of evenness and gloss, tends to smooth over the marked differences in the source materials, and even Davis seems constrained (and occasionally even flummoxed) by the horn. (Most of the tracks were recorded on Columbia's recently acquired two-track tape recorder.)[12] Ultimately the album is unsatisfactory, for Davis's playing was set off better by the roughness of Coltrane and the immediacy of a rhythm section than by the cushion of a big band, however sophisticated the arrangements and however propulsive the rhythms. This view has been shared by very few, for it was a big seller and has been acclaimed as a "masterpiece of jazz orchestration" by one critic and by other jazz musicians as "perfect" and "the greatest."[13] Whitney Balliett, however, insightful man that he is, described the music as "moony" and "saccharine."[14]

At the very end of 1957 Davis formed a quintet with Julian "Cannonball" Adderley, an alto saxophonist from Florida who had taken the New York nightclub scene by storm. Adderley was fluent—almost to the point of glibness—as well as spirited and joyful in his playing, even on the blues, at which he excelled. He was offered gigs both with Davis and with Gillespie, but accepted the former. He was two years younger than Davis and Coltrane, and he did not use drugs. He had enough to deal with as a diabetic. Davis described him as "a real nice guy on top of being an unbelievable alto player."[15]

By this time Coltrane had beaten his heroin habit and found religion, and for the rest of his life he devoted himself to spirituality and working on his music. He could be heard late at night after gigs practicing, and he even practiced during the breaks in the middle of gigs.[16] He played constantly, working out ideas, trying new harmonies, and perfecting his sound. Davis offered him his old job back, and Coltrane accepted. So did the members of what was now being called *The* Rhythm Section (Garland, Chambers, Jones). By the beginning of 1958, the old quintet was now a new sextet, and it didn't take long for them to appear in Columbia's recording studio to display their prowess.

The first recording of this new group was the justly famed *Milestones*, made in two sessions, one in early February and the other in early March 1958.[17] On the first track the group comes hurtling out of the gate on "Dr. Jekyll" at over 320 beats per minute. (This was Jackie McLean's "Dr. Jackle," which Davis had already recorded with McLean, Milt Jackson, Ray Bryant, Percy Heath, and Art Taylor in 1955.)[18] In fact, the whole twelve-measure tune (which the group plays twice at the outset) is over in nine seconds. Davis alternates hectic lines with shorter phrases (including what seems like a quote from "When the Saints Go Marching In"), the saxophones positively fly, the pianist plays echo games with the trumpet, the bass has a bowed solo, and the drummer takes a flailing couple of choruses. It is a startling announcement of a new combo; the fact that the three horns can play in unison on a tune this fast is a sign not only of the musicians' technical ability but also of their unanimity. In fact, Adderley and Coltrane already sound alike. The transitions between their traded choruses are so seamless that an inattentive listener can lose track of which man is playing when. But technical ability matters, too. It is astounding that these players can improvise fascinating musical lines when each chorus takes only nine seconds and when the chord changes occur sometimes at the rate of two per measure. The speed, the twisting and turning of the tune, and the facility of the solos suggest that Davis was sending a message with this first track: "You want bop? Here's bop!"

Already one can hear Davis, the great orchestrator, delighting in the exponentially increased number of possible solo arrangements with a sextet: "One voice can change the entire way a band hears itself. . . . It's a whole new thing when you add or take away a voice."[19] In this tune alone we have the following pattern: whole group playing the head—Davis's solo (ending with phrases traded with the drummer)—alternating saxophones for several choruses—bowed bass—return of Davis (starting with the echoes between trumpet and piano)—two choruses of drum solo—and the return of the whole group for the tail.

The next tune, "Sid's Ahead," features a rare appearance at the keyboard of the group leader, Miles Davis himself, who had learned some piano from Dizzy Gillespie. Apparently Garland was miffed at the lack of solo opportunities and walked out of the session. ("Sid's Ahead" was the last track recorded on the second session.) Davis comps behind the two other soloists, and it is amusing to hear him gradually loosen up over the course of the solos. (He has plenty of time to adapt to the role, for the piece lasts thirteen minutes.) The tune is a lovely relaxed swinging blues, apparently written by Davis himself. It is very much in the hard-bop style, with a blues basis and a very simple repeated figure, changing pitch over the chords. And here the solo order is also carefully thought out. Davis cedes the first spotlight to Coltrane, and takes his solo second, with Adderley third, thus placing the sound of the trumpet between that of the two saxophones. The solos are rounded off by a lengthy plucked bass outing by Chambers and some traded phrases between Davis and Jones on drums before the return of the head. Since the phrases of the tune are short, there are large areas of space in between them, which Chambers and Jones fill with deliciously swinging responses.

Closing out Side 1 was John Lewis's "Two Bass Hit," an interesting piece that had been recorded by Dizzy Gillespie's orchestra in 1947 and by Davis with Coltrane and the rest of the quintet in 1955 before Adderley joined them.[20] The tune is unusual but up-tempo and catchy, with a form something like ABBAC, and although it is actually a bit more complicated than that, it doesn't sound like it. The C section owes a lot to Thelonious Monk, with its short tritone-based snippets placed strategically in different places in the bar. The earlier quintet version was recorded by Columbia before Davis's contract with Prestige had expired and was not released until many years later. It was a showcase for Coltrane, with Davis (apart from the head and the tail) laying out until the last chorus, when he played a countermelody.[21] More or less the same pattern is followed here, except that both saxophone players take solos. Again the rich, expressive tone of Adderley's alto matches Coltrane's edgy tenor so well, and their fluency is sufficiently similar, that they are hard to tell apart. But Coltrane plays first, and Davis adds a clever descending chromatic countermelody to Adderley's last chorus. Both saxophonists slide in some cheeky quotes, but Adderley wins the quoting contest with references to Charlie Parker, George Gershwin, and some popular songs. Jones gets short but fiery drumming breaks. Garland gets almost nothing.

First on Side 2 came the title track, "Milestones," called just "Miles" on the original LP and referred to as such in the original liner notes by Charles Smith. This became one of Davis's favorite compositions to play in later years. It is also the second in a long string of titles after *Miles Ahead* to play games with Davis's eminently punnable first name.[22] The tune, again by Davis, is extremely catchy, comfortably up-tempo, though very simple indeed (see Example 3). It features eight bars of three short notes of the G-minor scale repeated (A). The B section is another eight bars of three notes of another scale, one step higher in A minor, also repeated (with a slight variant), but this time the notes are sustained. Then the A section returns. Significantly, from the point of view of what was to happen a year later on *Kind of Blue*, the harmony is static in each section. This is less apparent in the first section, because the bassist is walking the notes, than in the second, where he simply repeats the keynote throughout, as a kind of drone. The solos are arranged in yet another new order. As on "Sid's Ahead," Davis's trumpet separates the two saxophones, but this time Adderley plays first. For the first time on a Davis record, the producer decided to fade the ending. This track is rightly famous. It has been called "a perfect jazz performance."[23]

The next track is a trio-only performance for the rhythm section. Ahmad Jamal had recorded "Billy Boy" in 1951 on his album *Poinciana*. Here Garland gets to solo to his heart's content with his speedy take on the tune. The rhythm section, which seems a little underrecorded on the rest of the album, shines here, including a virtuoso and witty bowed solo from Chambers covering several choruses. Philly Joe Jones swings hard throughout and trades fiery fours with Garland in a veritable drumming primer before the return of the head. It seems that after an opportunity like this, it might be regarded as a little churlish of Garland to storm off the set before "Sid's Ahead." There are no other entire piano-trio performances on a Davis record. Again, Davis seems determined to mine the permutations of the combo in as many ways as possible.

Example 3. "Milestones" head (1958).

On the last track on Side 2 he finds yet one more pattern. For this piece he selects another Monk tune to match " 'Round Midnight," with which he had scored such signal success a year and a half earlier. "Straight, No Chaser" could have been composed by nobody else. Hard though it is to believe, formally and harmonically the piece is a straightforward, relaxed, medium-tempo 12-bar blues. And yet the short phrases of the melody cut directly across the standard four-bar groupings of the form like pick-up sticks on a chessboard. The solos start with the

Adderley-Davis-Coltrane order that worked so well on "Mile-stones," except that this time they are followed by two other soloists: piano first and then bass (plucked)—giving all five melody instruments a turn at the end of the album as though to display every one of them in a grand finale. (Philly Joe had just been featured on "Billy Boy.") And it is indeed grand, with everyone seeming to stretch out happily for several choruses and the whole track lasting nearly eleven minutes. It is slightly re-grettable that having discovered the effect of fade-out, Columbia couldn't leave well enough alone and so used it again to finish the side. However, it could be argued that the fading technique here leaves the impression that the musicians are reluctant to stop playing at all. And they do play four choruses at the end with such joy and commitment that we share their reluctance.

All the musicians in the sextet play "beyond themselves," as Davis intended. "I've always told the musicians in my band to play what they *know* and then play *above that.* Because then any-thing can happen, and that's where great art and music hap-pens."[24] Davis was yet again displaying his extremely fine sense of the overall sound of his group, manipulating the various com-binations of soloists, and particularly contrasting the *personali-ties* of the three horns: Coltrane's intensity, Adderley's fluidity, and his own spare style. The album has been called "one of the great classics of jazz."[25]

These albums significantly enhanced Davis's reputation and his income. He was fast becoming one of the most prominent members of the fashionable scene of the 1950s. As he remarked in his autobiography, "The group I had with Coltrane made me and him a legend." He dressed well, drove fast cars, squired attractive women, and drew members of the 1950s in-crowd—Marlon Brando, James Dean, Elizabeth Taylor, Ava Gardner, Frank Sinatra, Tony Bennett—to his club appearances.[26] He was a fa-mous figure in Europe, with Juliette Greco and Jean-Paul Sartre as friends, and articles about him appeared in British, Dutch, and German music magazines. He also had the unusual ability to appeal both to popular taste and to scholarly attention. He won prizes and popularity polls, his records started to sell well, and he was the subject of feature articles in *Time* (January 20, 1958) and *Life International* (August 11, 1958). *Time* dubbed him "the leader of the post-bop generation of blowers." On January 12, 1958, the *New York Times* had a photograph of Davis and several column inches devoted to him under the headline "Promising Jazz Talents Fulfilled"; a brief biography was put out by Columbia and published in *Down Beat;* he was interviewed and his music was discussed by jazz critics; and he was often one of the figures mentioned in the increasing number of books to be published about jazz during the 1950s. His personal intensity, whispering voice, curt manners, and stage deportment (he often faced his drummer instead of the audience) only added to the charisma. In the second half of the 1950s, for a number of the top jazz players, including Davis, their music began paying significant rewards. Dave Brubeck and Erroll Garner earned $3,000 a week in clubs and $2,500 for a concert, and the best sidemen could earn $20,000 a year for their work. Also, jazz was becoming more and more accepted both as artistic expression and as a phenomenon worthy of serious analysis precisely during the decade in which Davis was forging his personal style and making significant musical breakthroughs, seemingly every year.[27]

5. *Kind of Blue*

After the two recording sessions for *Milestones*, Davis replaced Red Garland as the group's pianist. Perhaps this decision was partly a result of the disagreement regarding "Sid's Ahead," but Davis was also looking for a new sound. He found it in the playing of Bill Evans, who was already making a name for himself in the jazz world. Evans had made a splash in George Russell's "All about Rosie" a year earlier, and Russell, who was working on a theory about the use of modes in jazz, recommended Evans to Davis. Evans played spaciously and had an advanced harmonic sense. His special sound was based on two technical features. He often played chords based on fourths instead of thirds, which produces a less grounded, more open texture, and he frequently omitted the root, or fundamental note, of chords, again creating a lighter, less earthbound effect. The lighter sound and less crowded manner were more akin to the understated way in which Davis himself played. "He plays the piano the way it should be played," said Davis about Bill Evans.[1] And for a man whose speech was as epigrammatic as his playing, and whose vocabulary was often sprinkled with blunt Anglo-Saxon expressions, Davis waxed poetic about Evans's playing: "Bill had this quiet fire. . . . [T]he sound he got was like crystal notes or sparkling water cascading down from some clear waterfall."[2] The admiration was mutual. Evans thought of Davis and the other musicians in his band as "superhumans."[3] Evans also fed Davis's fascination with classical music, introducing him to music by Ravel, Rachmaninov, Brahms, and Khachaturian.[4]

The choice of Evans shows once again how carefully Davis picked the players in his groups. Bill Evans was with Davis for only a few months, although, as we know, he was later persuaded to return for *Kind of Blue*. He grew tired of the traveling, and as the only white man in the band, he was often subject to racist comments and taunts from other black musicians and black audiences. But, as always, Davis was very clear on his own view: the music was all that mattered. "I have always just wanted the best players in my group, and I don't care about whether they're black, white, blue, red, or yellow."[5]

The drummer Philly Joe Jones also had to be let go, as his drug habit was making him unreliable. Davis replaced him with Jimmy Cobb, who was a great admirer of Jones's playing and had played with Cannonball Adderley before Adderley joined Davis's band. Cobb is a creative and sophisticated drummer, though not quite as driven as Jones, but with Evans in the group Davis tended to play softer pieces.[6]

But the next big project for Davis was not with the sextet but again with Gil Evans and a jazz orchestra. This time, the music was (mostly) taken from George Gershwin's *Porgy and Bess*. Many incentives seem to have combined to move Davis in this direction. Columbia was happy with the sales of *Miles Ahead*, their previous orchestral project with Davis and Gil Evans, and suggested the project to Davis; a new staging of the opera was touring nationwide and abroad; a movie version was in production; jazz versions of the music were frequently recorded, including a recent one by Ella Fitzgerald and Louis Armstrong; and Davis had a girlfriend, Frances Taylor (whom he later married), who was a dancer in the touring company of *Porgy*.[7]

The orchestra is almost as big as the *Miles Ahead* band, and Davis again plays flugelhorn on several tracks, but for several reasons the musical result here is somewhat more satisfactory. Gil Evans's arrangements are fresh. Also, bass and drums are more prominent, creating a far stronger sense of swing, and several instrumentalists other than Davis take solos. The tuba solo in "The Buzzard Song" is a delight. Philly Joe Jones (back for a guest appearance) is both controlled and powerful on "Gone." And how about that whooping French horn at the climax of "Prayer"? Davis exchanges flugelhorn for his trumpet on several numbers, immediately creating more variety in the timbre. His sound throughout is golden and deeply expressive. And let's face it, there are very few compositions that can match the musical masterpiece that is *Porgy and Bess*, which has served as a gold mine for jazz musicians since its premiere in 1935.

Trumpeter and Davis biographer Ian Carr says of *Porgy and Bess* that "the level of inspiration throughout . . . is exceptionally high: Miles plays as one possessed, and Evans writes with the same intensity."[8] The new Davis—both in his sextet and with a big band—did not please everyone. Ralph Ellison said that Davis (and Coltrane) had "gotten lost." Albert Murray, who doesn't like white people making jazz, said that all he could hear on *Porgy and Bess* was "a bunch of studio musicians playing decadent exercises in orchestration. . . . Gil Evans, my ass."[9]

But the variety of the album and the more thorough integration of soloist, small group, and big band make a considerably more effective recording than *Miles Ahead*, though one can never quite escape the oil-and-water impression provided by hearing

Davis with an orchestra. The album also established one more step on the way to *Kind of Blue*, because on one of the tracks ("I Loves You, Porgy") Gil Evans came up with the idea of using only two chords in the colorful orchestral opening and having Davis work off a single scale for his improvisation. The muted sound of Davis in this closed harmonic scheme certainly foreshadows the effect of the pensive "Blue in Green" from *Kind of Blue*.

All this goes to show that the modal music of *Kind of Blue* did not come out of a vacuum. As we have seen, Davis had already experimented with the idea of static harmony in "Milestones." He was naturally inclined toward the idea of more space in his music. And Bill Evans already utilized a playing technique that tended to float over the regular signposts of traditional harmony.

Just before the group went into the studio to record *Kind of Blue*, Davis had hired a new pianist to replace Bill Evans in the touring group. Wynton Kelly was a wonderfully gifted pianist, bluesy and right up on the beat, and a great supporter of soloists. Davis thought that he would be perfect for the group "because he was a combination of Red Garland and Bill Evans; he could play almost anything." Adderley described Kelly's strengths in similar language: He "does both the subdued things and the swingers very well. . . . Wynton is also the world's greatest accompanist for a soloist."[10] But the album had been planned around Bill Evans, and Davis and Evans had discussed the music for it for a while, so Evans came back for the recording and played on all the tracks except for one. Again it is a measure of the masterly way in which Davis chose his musicians that he asked Kelly to play on "Freddie Freeloader," the most conventional (blues) number on the album. The fact that Kelly was taken aback to see Bill Evans in the studio on the first day of recording may have influenced Davis's decision to record this track first.[11] It also may have influenced his decision to give Kelly the first solo on the track, to which Kelly responds with fine, clean bluesy playing, mostly right hand only. He fills in the holes of the melody, which is a relaxed, hard-bop tune of great simplicity, and his comping behind the soloists, especially behind Chambers (although the placement of the microphones gives the piano too much and the bass too little prominence) is unhurried and festooned with comfortable, traditional blues gestures.

For all the other pieces on *Kind of Blue*, the pianist was Bill Evans, and his sophisticated, contemplative sound colors the whole album. Even on the medium-tempo "So What" and "All Blues," his playing is essential to the music: light, rich, and blooming at the back of the beat rather than pushing the front of it. Indeed, Evans was a vital collaborator on the entire project. He had talked over many of the ideas for the album with Davis several weeks before the first recording session; he composed "Blue in Green" based on two chords that Davis had given him; he had met with Davis on the morning before the session; and he had written out the introduction to "So What" and all of the modes for "Flamenco Sketches" (either at that time or before the second session). Even though he was no longer officially in the group at the time, he played on both recording sessions.

The sessions were held about seven weeks apart, on March 2 and April 22, 1959.[12] The first was a double session, one in the afternoon and one in the evening. In the afternoon, they began with "Freddie Freeloader." Next came "So What," probably the most recognizable music associated with modal jazz (and Davis's contribution to it) the world over. Both of these tracks are about nine minutes long. In the evening, the group recorded the exquisite "Blue in Green," Bill Evans's composition and perhaps the most beautiful piece on the album. This is also the shortest track, at about five and a half minutes. In April, when the group reconvened, they recorded "Flamenco Sketches" first and then "All Blues." "Flamenco Sketches" runs about nine and a half minutes and "All Blues" about eleven and a half.

The final arrangement of the album has "So What" first, then "Freddie Freeloader," and finally "Blue in Green" on Side 1 and "All Blues" and then "Flamenco Sketches" on Side 2. Obviously there were practical reasons for this arrangement. Most LPs of the 1950s contained fifteen to twenty minutes per side, so accommodating the shorter "Blue in Green" together with the other tracks, all of which lasted between nine and eleven minutes, was not easy, and it was pushing the envelope to include it anyway. (In the end, Side 1 contained twenty-four minutes of music.) However, other arrangements would have been possible. What is more important is that the resulting order was clearly an artistic decision rather than a purely practical one. The opening of this new world had to be noticeable, so the more conventional blues "Freddie Freeloader" could not begin Side 1. On the other hand, one would not want to begin a program with a diffuse, dreamy kind of piece like "Blue in Green" or "Flamenco Sketches." As a result, "So What" is a perfect opening, as its immense popularity has later shown. Next on Side 1 came "Freddie Freeloader," sandwiched between the newer modal pieces, and the side closed in stillness with the remarkable "Blue in Green." Side 2 had only two tracks, opening with "All Blues" at a moderate tempo and again ending with floating, suspended music—the multimodal, very slow "Flamenco Sketches." Creating a program is an art in itself, and at least a part of the reason for the longevity and perennial appeal of *Kind of Blue* lies in its thoughtful arrangement of the music.

There is one element of this arrangement that is more prominent on the CD versions of the album than on the original LP. This element is the placement of "Blue in Green." On the CD, listeners are now presented with a continuous flow of music made up of five tracks. Of these, four are quite long, and they are placed two before and two after "Blue in Green." Regarding the program as a whole, therefore, one sees "Blue in Green" as the small capstone of a musical arch or as a gem in the center of a ring. This sense of circularity is mirrored in the music itself.

Bill Evans writes in his liner notes that "Blue in Green" is "circular" because it is based on a ten-measure repeating harmonic pattern. (This pattern starts off with the two chords that Davis had given Bill Evans to work on: G minor and A augmented.) But the entire form of the piece is also a circle or, more accurately, a palindrome. To put it succinctly, the order of events is piano solo, trumpet solo, piano solo, tenor sax solo, piano solo, trumpet solo, piano solo. Again, in shorthand: Piano-Trumpet-Piano-Sax-Piano-Trumpet-Piano. In this case the gem in the center is Coltrane, and a gem of a solo it is! It is marked by extraordinarily beautiful playing, as are the solos by Davis and Evans. But, as in all great art, complete symmetry is dull, and the palindrome is deliberately complicated by the following: the opening piano solo is not a complete chorus or even a five-measure half-chorus but a four-measure introduction; both trumpet solos last for two choruses; Evans plays double time on his second to last solo and stretches out the tempo on his last; and the piece ends with an additional two-measure tag. However, the sense of an arch form is strong, especially on a piece that takes its place at the top of the greater arch that is the album as a whole (see Figure 1).

The other tracks on the album once again show Davis's thoughtful approach to the organization and orchestration of his music. The order of soloists on "So What" is as follows: Davis, Coltrane, Adderley, Evans, Chambers. "Freddie Freeloader" begins with the piano: Kelly, Davis, Coltrane, Adderley, Chambers. "All Blues" reverses Coltrane and Adderley, placing Adderley directly after Davis: Davis, Adderley, Coltrane, Evans. And "Flamenco Sketches" has Davis soloing at both the beginning and the end: Davis, Coltrane, Adderley, Evans, Davis. Gil Evans was involved in the sessions,[13] although there is no record of what his influence might have been on the resulting music.

Figure 1. Arch form of "Blue in Green" within arch form of *Kind of Blue*.

The great strength of *Kind of Blue* lies in its collaboration among the players and the consistency of its inspiration, but a few highpoints deserve mention: these would include the Coltrane solo on "Blue in Green"; Davis's opening solo on "So What," in which he does so much with so little; Adderley's remarkable blues solo on "Freddie Freeloader"; Evans's playing throughout but especially on "Flamenco Sketches"; Chambers's amazing consistency on the vamp of "All Blues"; and two unforgettable moments out of a whole album full of felicities by Jimmy Cobb. One of these is the drum roll, preceded by shorter rolls, that comes between Coltrane and Adderley on "All Blues." The other is the cymbal crash that he produces on Davis's opening entrance for the first solo of "So What." It is as though he were announcing a whole new way of life.

There were many important musical events in 1959, and several significant records were released, but no event or recording matches the importance of the release of *Kind of Blue* on August 17, 1959. There were people waiting in line at record stores to buy it on the day it appeared.[14] It sold very well from its first day and received good reviews in the music magazines. *Metronome* found the playing "concise and pointed" and the ensemble "moving." *Down Beat* called the record "remarkable," "an album of extreme beauty and sensitivity," and ended its review by stating: "This is the soul of Miles Davis, and it's a beautiful soul."[15] In the early 1990s David Rosenthal wrote, "Thirty years after it was recorded, *Kind of Blue* remains, for many, Miles's greatest single achievement."[16] The album has sold increasingly well ever since. It is still selling thousands of copies a week and by now has probably sold over three million copies in the United States alone.[17] It is the best-selling jazz album in the Columbia Records catalogue, and at the end of the twentieth century it was voted one of the ten best albums ever produced.[18] The definition of a classic is something that is both of the highest excellence and of enduring significance. *Kind of Blue* is indubitably a classic.

6. "There Is No Justice"

The summer of 1959 saw the sextet performing at Birdland on Broadway and the Apollo Theater in Harlem, the Blackhawk club in San Francisco, and several summer festivals, including the new Playboy Jazz Festival in Chicago. (In September 1962 *Playboy* published its first in a long series of lengthy interviews with public figures. Its very first subject was Miles Davis.) At the end of August, the band was back at Birdland. And on August 26, at the peak of Miles Davis's career to date, disaster struck in the shape of a racist New York policeman. That night, during a break in the proceedings at the club, Davis walked a young white woman to a cab. A patrolman told him to move along, and Davis refused, pointing to his own name advertised on the marquee. During the confrontation a second policeman came up behind Davis and clubbed him repeatedly on the head with a nightstick. Davis was arrested, taken to the police station, and held overnight in jail. Pictures of Davis with his head bandaged and blood all over his shirt as well as outraged articles were in the papers the next day, and the arrest was soon ruled illegal. But the effect on Davis was long lasting. He wrote in his autobiography, "That incident changed me forever, made me much more bitter and cynical than I might have been." He had to conclude that "if you're black, there is no justice. None."[1]

It was clear nearly twenty years later that the incident had left deep psychic scars. In an interview with Sy Johnson in 1976 he said, "White people don't like me," and he referred to the fracas outside Birdland. "I mean a policeman grabbed me around the neck."—"Why?"—" 'Cause I was black." And in response to the question, "Is it gonna be okay?" Davis just shrugged. As to his street reputation, the beating did nothing but enhance it. Amiri Baraka (then LeRoi Jones) wrote later that "Miles was not only the cool hipster of our bebop youth, but now we felt he embodied the social fire of the times." In an affectionate piece published after his death, Gary Giddins said that the incident made him "a hero of the civil rights era."[2]

Davis was not the only black jazz musician to be beaten over the head by police. In 1945 pianist Bud Powell received the same treatment in Philadelphia, an event that may well have contributed to the mental breakdowns that plagued him for the rest of his life.[3] Also in the early 1940s drummer Art Blakey was savagely beaten by a policeman in Albany, Georgia. The injuries from this assault were only repaired by major surgery and the placement of a steel plate in Blakey's head.[4]

By the fall, the sextet was beginning to disintegrate. Cannonball Adderley left at the end of September. Coltrane was clearly itching to start his own band. He began telling other saxophone players and even the newspapers that he was leaving Davis. To keep him busy, Davis set him up with his own agent and manager. Coltrane also began playing with drummer Elvin Jones, who had been a friend of Davis since the early 1950s.[5] He did not make the final break until the spring of 1960, and even then Davis was able to tempt him back into the recording studio one more time in March 1961 (see chapter 7). Davis's last project of 1959 was based on a classical piece. He had heard a recording of Joaquin Rodrigo's guitar concerto, the *Concierto de Aranjuez*, while traveling on the West Coast, and he wanted to play some of the music. This turned into the next orchestral project with Gil Evans, who arranged the second movement of the concerto for a big band (two flutes, two oboes [one doubling clarinet], bass clarinet, bassoon, four trumpets, two trombones, three French horns, tuba, harp, bass, drums and percussion) and found some other Spanish-flavored pieces to fill out an LP. Again, like *Miles Ahead* and *Porgy and Bess*, the arrangements featured a kaleidoscope of shifting colors and textures against which the solo playing of Davis on both trumpet and flugelhorn could be highlighted. The recordings were made in two parts: the concerto in November 1959, and the rest of the album on two consecutive days in March 1960. The resulting record was *Sketches of Spain* (Columbia CL 1480).

Like all the Gil Evans collaborations, it is only partly successful, for the band plays neither with the precision of a classical orchestra nor with the loose freedom of a jazz band. With the concerto, one is left wondering what new light has been shed on the original, which is a superb piece, one of two excellent and colorful concertos for solo guitar and orchestra by Rodrigo. The *Concierto de Aranjuez* of 1939 established Rodrigo as one of the leading Spanish composers of his time; the *Fantasía para un gentilhombre*, also for solo guitar and orchestra and dating from 1954, conveys a similar sense of color, control, and atmosphere. (A much later guitar concerto, *Concierto para una fiesta*, is less successful and was written when Rodrigo was already in his eighties.) Evans uses only the slow movement of the *Aranjuez* concerto and takes considerable liberty in reorganizing the piece, which is unfortunate, for the original is extremely carefully gauged, balancing evocative, declamatory statements against placid passages. Davis plays beautifully, alternating flugelhorn and muted trumpet. Martin Williams, a gentle critic, wrote that the recording was "a failure, as . . . a comparison with any good performance of the movement by a classical guitarist would confirm."[6] The rest of the album is also variable. "Will o' the Wisp," completing Side 1, is another classical borrowing, this time from Manuel de Falla's ballet *El amor brujo,* written in 1915. De Falla represented the nationalist school of classical Spanish music for the first half of the twentieth century, as Rodrigo did for the middle and latter part of the century, and again Evans rewrites the original to accommodate a soloist and orchestral band. "The Pan Piper" has Davis representing a street vendor, much as he had done on the track "Strawberry and Devil Crab" on the *Porgy and Bess* album. "Saeta" is a moving example of Davis's solo playing, without the distraction of a constantly shifting orchestral texture, as the orchestra does little but sustain chords throughout, over muffled drums, which allows the listener to focus on Davis's flugelhorn and his direct, pained solo. A *saeta* is an Andalusian religious song sung by a woman alone on her balcony on Good Friday, as a procession, bearing statues of religious figures, pauses in the street beneath. It is both "joyous and sad," as Davis described it. It also carries the technique of modal playing beyond *Kind of Blue,* for it is based almost entirely on a single scale or mode. Finally, "Solea" is also melancholic, a flamenco gypsy lament, and according to Davis it is "a song about loneliness, about longing and lament. It's close to the American black feeling in the blues."[7] Davis chose to identify with what he saw as the "black" roots of both the last two tracks. But flamenco or "Eastern" scales predominate, and the entire album is colored not only by these melodic patterns but also by a pervasive use of "exotic" percussion instruments: castanets, tambourines, maracas. Jack Chambers points out how on "Solea" the two drummers, Jimmy Cobb and Elvin Jones, play contrasting rhythms, one marking the flamenco rhythm on snare, the other playing jazz shuffle on a ride cymbal. "The contending rhythms quite literally embody the musical forces at play throughout *Sketches of Spain*."[8]

The album also incorporates more of Teo Macero than previous recordings. Macero says that he tried "a lot of new tricks" on this recording, made possible by the new techniques of stereo recording. "We had the bands going off the side and one band going in the middle and then coming back and splitting it and going to the sides again." He also did a great deal of editing and tape splicing, an activity that may be responsible for some of the unsatisfactory feeling of *Sketches* and one that made him (controversially) much more than just a producer for some of the Miles Davis recordings of the late 1960s. Macero is an accomplished studio technician, but he is also a composer, a saxophone player, and a Guggenheim Foundation award winner. Over his career he has composed prolifically, producing jazz as well as classical compositions, arrangements, ballet scores, and film and television scores. He was the principal jazz producer for Columbia. As he stressed to me in my interview with him, he spent more time working closely with Davis than anyone else; he regards him as a "genius."[9]

With *Sketches of Spain*, the projects of the 1950s came to an end for Miles Davis. Looking back over the decade from 1949 to 1959, one can see that Miles Davis had accomplished remarkable achievements. Beginning as an unknown and hesitant sideman, he had become one of the most famous international figures in jazz. He was rich and happily married. He was recognized as a fashion plate, a hipster, an icon of "cool." He had traveled to Europe and had appeared at the important jazz festivals that were springing up around the United States. He had led performing groups that featured (and nurtured) some of the greatest jazz musicians of his time. Indeed, he had discovered and "made" some of the greatest jazz musicians of his time. He had created dozens of recordings that continued to sell (and bring in royalties) and carry his name further and further afield. Among them were masterpieces of small-group jazz—*Bags' Groove*, the "apostrophe" albums for Prestige, *'Round about Midnight*, *Milestones*, and *Kind of Blue*—as well as "concerto" albums that featured Davis's solo playing against an orchestral background—*Miles Ahead*, *Porgy and Bess*, and *Sketches of Spain*—which were popular if not always musical successes. He had helped to create three new stylistic movements in jazz: cool, hard bop, and modal. The decade had begun well (*Birth of the Cool*), entered a major three-year slump (heroin addiction), and then gone from strength to strength.[10]

The new decade was also to begin with a slump. In part this was due to the shadow (and who knows what psychic and physical damage) of the vicious assault on him on the sidewalks of New York in August 1959. What a humiliating, frightening, and enraging experience it must be to stand at the peak of one's career only to be reminded, suddenly, unexpectedly, and brutally, that the mere color of one's skin can at any time prompt a smashing of one's dreams. Davis was "put in his place" by an ignorant, racist bully wearing the uniform of law and order. That Davis's slump lasted for only a few years; that he was not brutalized by the experience; that he could continue to work with white men; that he could continue to work at all: these are things for which all of us should be grateful. It is particularly poignant that in the spring of the year, after the conclusion of the *Kind of Blue* recording sessions and before the attack, Miles was feeling "on top of the world."[11] But apart from this appalling setback there were additional reasons for the next period of artistic stagnation, as we shall see.

7. Not Happening

The early 1960s for Davis were marked by several years of floundering, with regard to both personnel and musical direction.
Some of the music produced by this floundering is wonderful,
and some of it seems aimless and lost. I have outlined in previous chapters the challenges faced by Davis after the high point
of 1959 and *Kind of Blue:* the encroachment of rock music on the
popular imagination; the shock waves produced by Ornette
Coleman and the other exponents of free jazz; Davis's physical
ailments; the attack outside Birdland. But the greatest challenge
to confront Davis in the early 1960s was the departure from his
group of John Coltrane.

Of the great sextet of the late 1950s, Cannonball Adderley
was the first to go, leaving in September 1959. And after talking
about it for over a year, offering his job to other players, and
openly setting himself apart from his colleagues on their final
tour together (to Europe), Coltrane finally left to form his own
quartet in May 1960.[1] This move had a profound effect on

Coltrane's own music making, as his subsequent recordings show.[2] But its effect on Miles Davis was perhaps even more profound.[3] It took Davis many years to recover from the loss, and as I shall show, his recovery was partly due to his emulation of the new musical concepts realized by Coltrane's new group. Even as many as ten years later, Davis would refer ruefully to Coltrane as having had the abilities of "five tenor players."[4] Davis's rhythm section, made up of Wynton Kelly, piano, Paul Chambers, bass, and Jimmy Cobb, drums, quit at the end of 1962.

This artistic slump lasted for five years, 1960–65, and though there are some fine musical moments, Davis's dissatisfaction and disillusionment at this time are clearly represented by three elements: the search for a new saxophone player, the paucity (and erratic quality) of the recordings, and Davis's demeanor. The last is well documented: Davis was surly, rude to his audience, often playing very little at his own gigs, and was (revealingly) particularly caustic about the revolutionaries who were forming the jazz vanguard in his place.[5] Of Ornette Coleman, Davis said: "Hell, just listen to what he writes and how he plays it . . . the man is all screwed up inside."[6] When he went to hear Cecil Taylor, Davis "just cursed and walked out."[7] And in a blindfold test in *Down Beat*, he commented that Eric Dolphy played "like somebody was standing on his foot."[8]

The man who had played with Charlie Parker at the age of twenty-one, who had been blazing new trails for jazz over the past decade, and who had forged an immediately identifiable and unique personal style, found himself without direction for the first time in his life.[9] In 1961 he was happily married, and he felt good about his home life, but "the music wasn't going too good for me during this period. . . . [T]he music wasn't happening and that was fucking me up. I was starting to drink more than I had in the past, and I was taking pain medication for the sickle-cell anemia. And I was starting to use more coke, I guess because of the depression."[10] By 1964 Davis was beginning to be regarded as a figure of the past. This attitude is typified by a long article in the thirtieth-anniversary issue of *Down Beat* summarizing Davis's career. It was, significantly, entitled "Miles and the 1950s."[11] Miles himself recalled, "A whole lot of younger players and critics jumped down my throat . . . called me 'old-fashioned' and shit."[12]

In 1962 Davis's father died suddenly at the age of sixty, which devastated him, as he had not been able to pay him a final visit. And in September of that same year, it became clear that the Birdland incident still lay heavily on Davis's mind. His interview with Alex Haley for *Playboy*, uncharacteristically for Davis, focused entirely on race.[13] In February 1964 he suffered another shock when his mother died. And in that same year, his wife Frances, tired of Davis's moodiness, his abusive behavior, and his overuse of alcohol and cocaine, finally left him.

The two other elements in the musical story, the search for a new saxophone player and the small number and variable quality of the recordings, can be sketched jointly. From Coltrane's departure in May 1960 to the hiring of Wayne Shorter in September 1964, Davis hired and fired (or lost) seven saxophonists: Jimmy Heath, tenor, who was about the same age as Davis, talented but not innovative, and who played with him for two months in the summer of 1960; Sonny Stitt, alto and tenor, also about the same age, also fairly set in his ways, who was with Davis for several months; Hank Mobley, tenor, regarded as "straightforward" and "workmanlike,"[14] with Davis for a year; Rocky Boyd, tenor, about whom little is known, who was only in the Davis band briefly, leaving in early 1962; Frank Strozier, alto, who overlapped from late 1962 to early 1963 with George Coleman, tenor, a somewhat more adventurous but occasionally awkward player, who stayed with Davis until the spring of 1964; and finally Sam Rivers, tenor, more experimental than any of the others but not to Davis's liking, who left the quintet in August 1964.

The number of studio recordings from this period is remarkably small: *Someday My Prince Will Come* was recorded in March 1961, *Quiet Nights* in July and August 1962, and *Seven Steps to Heaven* in April and May 1963.[15] These were the only studio albums issued until the beginning of 1965, when the new quintet had coalesced sufficiently to make its first recording. Columbia was forced to make up the deficiency by issuing live recordings, and of course some of these have since become celebrated—the Blackhawk and Carnegie Hall performances, for example, both from 1961, as well as the concert at Philharmonic Hall in February 1964.[16] Live recordings from Antibes (July 1963), Tokyo (July 1964), and Berlin (September 1964) on French CBS, Sony (Japan), and CBS Germany, respectively, are much less known in the United States.[17] This is a pity, for the Tokyo performance of "My Funny Valentine," for example, is the most beautiful and heartfelt (as well as the least known) version of this tune that Davis ever recorded.[18] But for the prolific Davis, three studio recordings in nearly five years was a poor showing indeed. (In the previous five years, he had released twelve studio albums.)

A review of these albums will also show that Miles Davis's musical direction was still uncertain. In addition it will show how much he was still looking to John Coltrane. *Someday My Prince Will Come* is by far the most impressive of the three. It uses Hank Mobley, who would later go on to record some of the classics of hard bop and who acquits himself admirably on this album despite the faint praise of his reviewers,[19] but more significantly it also brings back Coltrane himself for two of the items, including the title track. I would even like to suggest that Davis's choice of the tune "Someday My Prince Will Come" for this album may have been influenced by Coltrane. The success of Coltrane's "My Favorite Things,"[20] which is based on a widely known song in waltz meter, must have impressed Davis and encouraged him to make his own contribution based on parallel material: another widely known song, which is also in waltz meter.

"My Favorite Things" came from the Broadway musical *The Sound of Music*, the final collaboration between composer Richard Rodgers and lyricist Oscar Hammerstein II, which opened on Broadway on November 16, 1959, starring Mary Martin and Theodore Bikel. "Someday My Prince Will Come" was a favorite song in the enormously popular Disney movie *Snow White and the Seven Dwarfs*, which premiered in 1937 at New York's Radio City Music Hall and was America's first full-length animated feature film. Coltrane's recording was released in March 1961; Davis went to the studio to record his in the same month of the same year.

The second album of the three, *Quiet Nights* (1962), is an unmitigated disaster. Trying vainly to capitalize on the new bossanova craze, the record is static, pale, very short, and thoroughly unsatisfactory.[21] It should not have been released: Gil Evans, who was the arranger, blamed the company; Davis blamed the producer.[22] But with Davis so unproductive, one can understand Columbia's overeagerness.[23]

Seven Steps to Heaven (1963) contains some fine music, though it is not well unified. Three of the six tracks were recorded in California, three in New York, with different pianists and drummers in each location. The California tracks are muted ballads, the New York ones up-tempo and open horn. George Coleman is the tenor player. Of particular note is the makeup of the New York combo: for the first time, Herbie Hancock, Ron Carter, and Tony Williams join Davis in the studio. These men were to form the nucleus of the new quintet. Davis's excitement is palpable in the music of those tracks ("Seven Steps to Heaven," "So Near, So Far," and "Joshua"). He plays experimentally and with energy. It is precisely to this time that his comment "I knew right away that this was going to be a motherfucker of a group" refers, and his autobiography continues: "For the first time in a while I found myself feeling excited inside, because if they were playing that good in a few days, what would they be playing like in a few months?"[24] Particularly notable is the contribution of Tony Williams, who was seventeen years old but whose crisp brilliance drives the whole ensemble. It was sixteen months before the last piece of the puzzle would be in place. Wayne Shorter joined in the fall of 1964, fitting into the group "like a hand in a glove," as Herbie Hancock has said.[25] It was only four months later, after touring in California and Europe, that the group was in the studio to make *E.S.P.*, the first of their six studio recordings together.[26] (A summary list and chronology of the recordings, both studio and live, of Davis's groups from the departure of Coltrane in May 1960 to the making of *E.S.P.* in January 1965 is given in Table 1.)

E.S.P. was a beginning and an important one. Scott Yanow called it "a total break from the past," and Jack Chambers writes that *E.S.P.* "served notice . . . of a change of direction."[27] The direction was one that would be perfectly achieved in *Miles Smiles*. Forms, tempos, and meters are freer, all the compositions are new, and the band members themselves are the featured composers.[28] The dedication and intensity of the music on *Miles Smiles* and the other albums of 1965–68 derive from Davis's new vision, a sudden understanding of a way forward, one that did not completely follow the old conventions of bop or the apparently formless freedom of the new jazz. The vision was inspired by his new band members, and it was one that would result in a new style, one to which we can apply the term *post bop*. The excitement of the music also comes from a renewed musical commitment on the part of Miles Davis, a personal breakthrough from a period of disenchantment and lost bearings.

Of the six albums recorded by this cohesive and probing new group, the first is an announcement, the second (*Miles Smiles*) is a high point, while the third (*Sorcerer*) ranges from uninspired ("Pee Wee") to brilliant ("Vonetta").[29] *Nefertiti*, the fourth of the set, has received mixed reviews: Jack Chambers writes that it "rivals [*Miles Smiles*] as a showcase of this quintet's

Table 1. Recordings, both studio and live, made by Miles Davis between May 1960 and January 1965. (Live albums are asterisked. Names of new personnel are in boldface.)

Date	Album	Personnel	Catalogue
October 1960	*Miles Davis and Sonny Stitt: Live in Stockholm 1960**	Miles Davis, **Sonny Stitt** (as/ts), **Wynton Kelly** (p), Paul Chambers (b), Jimmy Cobb (dr)	Dragon DRLP 129/130
March 1961	*Someday My Prince Will Come*	Davis, **Hank Mobley** (ts), Kelly, Chambers, Cobb; with Coltrane on two tracks	Columbia CS 8456
April 1961	*Friday Night at the Blackhawk; Saturday Night at the Blackhawk**	Davis, Mobley, Kelly, Chambers, Cobb	Columbia 44257 and 44425
May 1961	*Miles Davis at Carnegie Hall: More Music from the Legendary Carnegie Hall Concert**	Davis, Mobley, Kelly, Chamber, Cobb; Gil Evans and His Orchestra	Columbia CS 8612 CBS 460064
July 1962/ April 1963	*Quiet Nights*	Davis, **George Coleman** (ts), **Victor Feldman** (p), **Ron Carter** (b), **Frank Butler** (dr); Gil Evans and His Orchestra	Columbia CS 8906
April/May 1963	*Seven Steps to Heaven*	Davis, Feldman, Carter, Butler; Davis, Coleman, **Herbie Hancock** (p), Ron Carter (b), **Tony Williams** (dr)	Columbia CL 2051
June 1963	*Miles in St. Louis**	Davis, Coleman, Hancock, Carter, Williams	VGM Records 0003
July 1963	*Miles Davis in Europe**	Davis, Coleman, Hancock, Carter, Williams	Columbia CS 8993
February 1964	*Four and More: Recorded Live in Concert**	Davis, Coleman, Hancock, Carter, Williams	Columbia CL 2453
February 1964	*My Funny Valentine: Miles Davis in Concert**	Davis, Coleman, Hancock, Carter, Williams	Columbia CL 2306
July 1964	*Miles in Tokyo**	Davis, **Sam Rivers** (ts), Hancock, Carter, Williams	CBS-Sony SOPL 162
September 1964	*Miles in Berlin**	Davis, **Wayne Shorter** (ts), Hancock, Carter, Williams	CBS S 62976
January 1965	*E.S.P.*	Davis, Shorter, Hancock, Carter, Williams	Columbia CS 9150

achievements," whereas Ian Carr finds it cerebral, self-conscious, and less than satisfying.[30] Both writers, however, admire the title track, which sets up a tension between chromaticism and tonality, repetition and change, group and individual, and between the prearranged and the spontaneous. The last two albums, *Miles in the Sky* and *Filles de Kilimanjaro*, are those in which Davis first begins to experiment with electric instruments and with the addition of other players to the group. In this sense, therefore, they signal "the beginning of the end" of this great quintet.[31]

8. The Second Quintet

Miles Davis, Wayne Shorter, Herbie Hancock, Ron Carter, and Tony Williams entered the Columbia studio on 30th Street in New York City on October 24, 1966. Their last visit to a recording studio (in Hollywood, California, for *E.S.P.*) had been twenty-one months earlier, in January 1965. During the time of Davis's illness, surgeries, and slow recovery, recordings were made of the group only three times: over the course of two nights at the Plugged Nickel in Chicago in December 1965; on a visit to Portland State College in Portland, Oregon, on May 21, 1966 (with Richard Davis sitting in for Ron Carter); and at the Newport Jazz Festival on July 4, 1966. The group made appearances in Philadelphia, Detroit, New York, and Washington, D.C., at the end of 1965 (but again with other bassists) and several times at the Village Vanguard and other venues in 1966 as a complete ensemble with Ron Carter. But there were no studio recordings made during this time.

Miles Davis was clearly the senior member of this group. By October 1966, he was forty years old. Shorter was thirty-three, Carter twenty-nine, Hancock twenty-six, and Williams only twenty. But although they were young, these musicians were by no means inexperienced.

Wayne Shorter in particular was beginning to show the jazz world what a brilliant and prolific composer and performer he was. He was a patrician choice for Davis, who had already experimented with many other tenor players, as we have seen. Shorter and Davis had even cut a few tracks together in August 1962.[1] Miles hired Shorter away from Art Blakey's Jazz Messengers, where he was music director (i.e., composer and arranger) and had played since 1959.[2] By autumn of 1966, he had already recorded six albums as leader of his own group: *Night Dreamer, Juju, Speak No Evil, The Soothsayer* (all 1964), *The All-Seeing Eye* (1965), and *Adam's Apple* (1966)—featuring twenty-two of his own compositions.

By the time Ron Carter joined Davis, he had performed, toured, and recorded with Eric Dolphy, Don Ellis, Randy Weston, Jaki Byard, Bobby Timmons, and Cannonball Adderley. He was so much in demand in New York and had so many commitments already that he was not even able to accompany the Miles Davis Quintet on its early tours.

By 1966 Herbie Hancock had recorded four albums as leader: *Takin' Off* (1962), which included the instantly popular and influential hard-bop piece "Watermelon Man," *My Point of View* (1963), *Empyrean Isles* (1964) with the hard-bop classic "Cantaloupe Island," and *Maiden Voyage* (1965).[3] He was known for his phenomenal piano technique as well as for the originality of his composing voice.

The twenty-year-old Tony Williams had already been performing professionally for some years. His most important association before Davis was with Jackie McLean. He began playing with Davis in 1963 (on *Seven Steps to Heaven*) and had released two recordings as leader of his own group before 1966: *Lifetime* (1964) and *Spring* (1965).[4] Davis was particularly excited about Williams. He wrote in his autobiography about first hearing him play: "I had heard this great little seventeen-year-old drummer . . . named Tony Williams, who just blew my fucking mind he was so bad. . . . Man, just hearing that little motherfucker made me excited all over again. . . . I could definitely hear right away that this was going to be one of the baddest motherfuckers who had ever played a set of drums." And he added, "Tony was always the center that the group's sound revolved around."[5]

The musical training of several of the players in this quintet was quite formal. Davis, as is well known, came to New York in 1944 to study at Juilliard. Although he spent most of his time on 52nd Street and hanging out with Charlie Parker, he studied with symphonic players, took piano lessons, and did not quit Juilliard until a year later.[6] Wayne Shorter attended New York University from 1952 to 1956, receiving his bachelor's degree in music education. Herbie Hancock was a child prodigy who began studying the piano at the age of seven and performed the first movement of Mozart's Piano Concerto No. 26 in D Major, K. 537, with the Chicago Symphony Orchestra when he was eleven. He graduated from Grinnell College in Iowa in 1960 with degrees in electrical engineering and musical composition.[7] Ron Carter began studying the cello at the age of ten and switched to double bass at seventeen. He studied double bass at the Eastman School of Music, where he played in the Philharmonia Orchestra, earning his bachelor of music degree in 1959. In 1961 he earned a master's degree from the Manhattan School of Music. The only member of the quintet not to receive advanced classical training was Tony Williams, who grew up surrounded by jazz: his father was a saxophonist who took him to the jazz clubs in Boston throughout his childhood. He studied with Alan Dawson, Art Blakey, and Max Roach and was playing professionally by the time he was fifteen.

When the group played together, Davis worked to create circumstances that would encourage spontaneity, experimentation, and immediacy. "[Miles] was the only bandleader who paid his personnel not to practice at home," said Wayne Shorter. "He always wanted it fresh."[8] In his autobiography Davis spoke about how he deliberately created this atmosphere: "See, if you put a musician in a place where he has to do something different from what he does all the time . . . [h]e has to use his imagination, be more creative, more innovative . . . [b]ecause then anything can happen, and that's where great art and music happens."[9] This spontaneity was by no means undermined—on the contrary it was enhanced—by the kind of intellectual preparation undertaken by the rhythm section, who worked really hard once they began playing for Miles. Carter recalled that early on they were playing two gigs a night (six hours) and that afterwards he, Hancock, and Williams would go to an all-night cafeteria and sit together talking for hours "trying to understand and analyze as best we could what took place and to have a clearer view of it to work on . . . for tomorrow night."[10]

This kind of freshness is evident even on the studio recordings. On *Miles Smiles,* for example, there are several indicators of how alive and spontaneous were the performances. First, the studio tapes show that every single track is a first complete take. The band would rehearse the head. If the head came together properly, and Davis was satisfied with the beginning of his solo (he always solos first), the performance continued, and that was the take.[11] Second, the number of flubs, wrong entries, uncertainty, and poor ensemble conveys the distinct ambiance of live performance. "When they make records with all the mistakes in," Davis said during his first live recording dates at the Blackhawk in San Francisco in April 1961, "then they'll really make jazz records."[12]

9. The Album *Miles Smiles*, Side 1

Miles Smiles features three compositions by Wayne Shorter ("Orbits," "Footprints," and "Dolores"), one by Davis ("Circle"), and two by composers not in the quintet: "Freedom Jazz Dance" by Eddie Harris and "Ginger Bread Boy" by Jimmy Heath. None of the other albums of the Second Quintet contains music by composers outside the group.[1] The Harris and Heath numbers are catchy and up-tempo. "Freedom Jazz Dance" in particular has a funky, hard-bop feel (and, after Davis's recording, it became a standard). Both are perfect foils for the Davis and Shorter pieces, which are far more abstract in conception. The fact that three of the tunes—"Footprints," "Freedom Jazz Dance," and "Ginger Bread Boy"—had been recorded earlier provided the perfect opportunity for Davis to demonstrate how radically new was his conception of the music.

The album contains four fast numbers (three of them extremely fast and one of them just up-tempo), one very slow waltz,

(Fast Swing)

Example 4. "Orbits" head from *Miles Smiles* (1966).

and one spacious tune in 6/4 meter. They are distributed on the album so that the tempo on Side 1 moves from very fast to very slow to broad, and on Side 2 from very fast to just fast to extremely fast.

The album opens with Shorter's "Orbits" (see Example 4). This is a highly original work.[2] Its atmosphere is one of dislocation and eeriness (perhaps this gave rise to the title), resulting from its avoidance of conventional form, unusual phrase lengths, odd gearing of the phrases against the measure, undulating melody shapes, fragmentary gestures, internal repetitions, and "spacey" harmony.

The music of the head falls into two sections, the first of nine measures, the second of twenty. The first section is made from a three-measure phrase, which is then shortened to two measures, and a four-measure close, which incorporates an even more compressed (one-measure) version of the phrase and a descending cadence. The harmony slides from C to G, and the melody stresses a tritone (G and D$^\flat$). The sense of hurtling disruption is created by the tempo (approximately 260 beats per minute), foreshortening of the phrase length (three measures instead of four, truncated to two and then one), the elision of the end of measure 3 into measure 4 (the end of the first phrase into the second), and the compression of the opening gesture in measure 7. Significant notes in the tune hover over the harmony rather than locking in with it (e.g., the opening A over C, and the D$^\flat$ over G), adding to the "spacey" quality. This is also accomplished by the moment of timelessness at the cadence, the extra measure (either measure 6 or measure 9), and the half-note triplets.

Contributing to the atmosphere are the bass and drums (the piano is silent). While the horns play in tight unison and are crisply articulated (Davis on open horn, Shorter back from the mike), bass and drums hit sparse irregular accents during the two statements of the opening phrase and, except for a muted roll and an anticipatory G$^\flat$ in the bass, lay out during the closing four measures (see Example 5).

Drums and bass also serve to divide the second section of the head into two parts (see Example 4 again). They treat the first six measures of this section (measures 10–15) like the opening; that is, they play during the first two measures and then lay out for the next four, giving a cadential feeling to measure 15, which is enhanced by the long note (F). At measure 16 they both begin

Example 5. Bass and drums on opening section of "Orbits" head.

to play a fairly regular four-beat, the bass walking fast. Against this division, the phrases of the tune push for unity. One hears a more regular phrase structure than in the first section: two wave-shaped four-measure phrases, each ending on the pitch C (measures 10–13 and 16–19.) The second of these is a modified sequence of the first, displaced rhythmically at its outset by an eighth note and pitched a fourth higher over a parallel progression. The first of these phrases has a two-measure ending tag (measures 14–15), reaching the long F mentioned above. The second also has a two-measure ending tag (measures 20–21), but this one imparts a greater sense of closure because of its definitive locking on to the beat (the first phrase in the piece to do this) and its arrival at the pitch C, echoing the C two measures earlier. This tag is itself followed by a further two-measure close, reaching the C an octave lower. Here closure is further enhanced by the lower pitch. The process is repeated and affirmed in measures 24–29 (tag + close + repeat of close).

In this second section, the tonal rationale of the piece becomes clearer. The melodic goal of the music is C (see measures 13, 19, 21, 23, 25, 27, and 29), confirming the cadence at the end of the first section. The harmonic goal sounds like F. Much of the melody circles (orbits?) the key of F rather than inhabiting it completely. This effect is significantly enhanced by the absence of the piano and the nonharmonic walking of the bass, thus giving unusual weight to the harmonic implications of the melody.

This pattern of melody and harmony is not straightforward. This does not stop Miles Davis from soloing intensely and creatively, however. He takes more than two choruses but less than three, for the third is truncated and focuses increasingly on the cadential phrases at the end of the second section. Davis's playing is fast, of extended range, filled with melodic fragments of the tune, and closely tailored to the harmony. His elastic treatment of the form is followed with breathtaking precision by Carter and Williams. Carter is running quarters, which frees Williams to color and splash on tom-toms and cymbals. Rolls are used both as signals of (shifting) structural points and as independent punctuation.

Shorter's solo is freer than Davis's. His playing also covers less than three choruses, but his stretching of the form, though it continues throughout, starts right at the beginning of his solo, when he echoes Davis's closing gestures. (This nod in the direction of the previous soloist also occurs between Hancock and Shorter.)[3] Shorter's greater familiarity with the tune (as its composer) is evident in the ease with which he negotiates the patterns, the fluency of his playing, and the freedom he employs in expanding brief phrases from the head. Williams is similarly inspired to more frequent and more irregular patterns for Shorter's solo, and he plays more on high hat and ride cymbal than on drums for a lighter sound in keeping with the saxophone timbre.[4]

Perhaps the most remarkable solo is Herbie Hancock's. The piano has been silent up to this point, and Hancock now plays a fleet, brilliant solo with right hand only. This produces a special, fresh effect (and the piano is miked much more closely than it was for *E.S.P.*). Hancock acknowledges Shorter's closing gesture

(Rim of snare)

etc.

Example 6. Rhythmic pattern throughout "Orbits."

as he starts, and the fluency and inventiveness of his ideas are riveting. He touches the tune only at the beginning and end of his solo, and at the end he returns once more to the closing gesture as interpreted by Shorter. Bass and drums stay light and agile throughout, with the bass entering the higher register for several passages. Tony Williams concentrates on the higher colors of his instruments, barely touching bass drum or floor tom. Apart from the beginning and the end, he is tapping on the rim of his snare drum with a quasi-*clave* pattern throughout, which is also circular and which provides great drive and energy as the ear keeps wanting to align the asymmetrical rhythm with the beat (see Example 6).

A roll reintroduces the head, although the horns play only the second section. The ensemble is scrappy, the bass misses a cue, the horns differ on the number of extra statements of the cadential gesture, and the bass overlaps the drums by a couple of measures, but the tune is so unusual, the mutuality of feeling is so strong, and the solos are so capable and above all so different, it was no wonder they called it a wrap. A schematic representation of the events in "Orbits" and on the other five tracks on *Miles Smiles* is given in Figure 2.

The theme of circularity is carried through to the second piece on the first side of the album, "Circle," though in most respects there could not be more contrast between the two. "Circle" is slow, moody, modal, and in 3/4 time. It is also harmony-based, drawing meaning from the color and juxtaposition of harmonic *areas*, whereas the previous track derives much of its significance from the shape, structure, content, and harmonic implications of its melody.

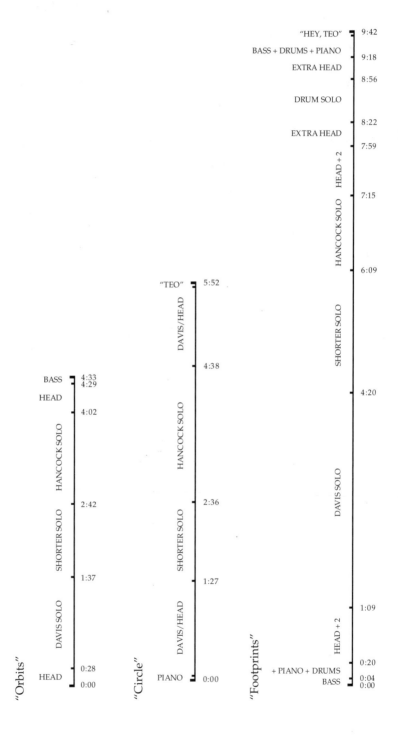

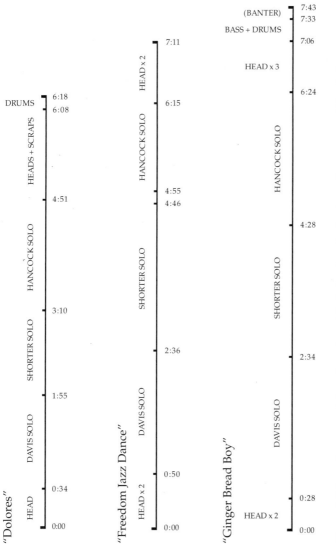

Figure 2. Schematic representation of events and their durations in the six performances on *Miles Smiles*.

Anthony Tuttle called "Circle" "a sophisticated ballad"; Chambers writes that it is "decidedly a ballad (by any definition) although not exactly a song (by the formal definition)."[5] Perhaps we would be better off circumscribing the reach of this word. *The New Grove Dictionary of Jazz* defines ballad as "a slow, sentimental love song . . . generally cast in 32-bar song form." And it continues: "The word is often used, loosely, of any slow piece, regardless of its form, style, or subject matter." Using it loosely, then, would cause us to sweep "Circle," several of the pieces on *Kind of Blue*, " 'Round Midnight," and many other Davis performances into the ballad category, although I think that doing so would obscure many of their unique properties.

"Circle" is certainly reminiscent of "So What," "Blue in Green," and "Flamenco Sketches" from *Kind of Blue* as well as of "Drad-Dog" from *Someday My Prince Will Come,* although it is the only waltz among them.[6] The tempo is approximately dotted half note = 48 beats per minute. Its modal quality is evident from the outset, as against a static background (slowly changing harmonies, piano comping discreetly and mostly on the beat, brushes, significant tones from the bass) Davis plays the tune Harmon-muted with long notes and expressive pauses. Frank Tirro has described this track as "one of the great performances of the decade."[7]

The piece has two sections (see Example 7): a first, which is made up of ten measures and moves (circuitously and colorfully) from D minor to E minor, and a second, which is elastic, that is, it has fixed elements at its beginning, middle, and end, but it can be compressed or stretched. The fixed elements of the second section are the first four measures, which move from E minor (through $A^\flat$) back to D minor, a central passage that goes to $D7\flat5$, and the last four measures that home in on the dominant (via the substitute dominant $E^\flat$) in order to prepare the return of D minor at the beginning of the tune. In this way, the composition is constructed as a "circle."

Example 7. "Circle" head from *Miles Smiles* (1966).

Davis is listed as the composer of this piece, and perhaps this partially explains the sophistication of his note choices in the opening melody: G# over D augmented in measure 6, for example, or the B natural over Asus4 in measures 14 and 15. Perhaps one could think of this opening as the first solo rather than as the head. Davis plays alone, not in unison with Shorter, and the long pause and the fragmentary nature of the melody in the second section suggest improvisation rather than precomposition. This, too, brings "Circle" closer in line with "Blue in Green," "Flamenco Sketches," and "Drad-Dog," all of which feature slow tempos, modal harmonies, and Davis playing alone, with Harmon mute, at the outset.

After the opening, Davis plays two further smoldering choruses, keeping to the initial template exactly. However, when Shorter solos, he both expands and contracts the second section.

Hancock plays the most freely: his account of the second section ranges from eight to twenty measures. All soloists, however, keep the first section to exactly ten measures. Of course, soloists are so used to making phrases of eight measures that at the end of Shorter's first improvisation over the first section one can hear him heading for an ending after eight, only to recuperate adroitly for the extra two measures.

The elegance and coherence of Hancock's solo (see Example 8) have led more than one commentator to compare it to the work of a classical composer. On the LP jacket, Anthony Tuttle writes of a "beautifully wrought expression of simple lyricism that at times seems to echo both Chopin and Debussy." Bob Belden regards it as "one of the most remarkable solos in the history of jazz. Improvised, yet balanced with ideas and executed with the grace of a concert pianist performing Chopin or Rachmaninoff."[8]

Of course, what makes the solo remarkable is that it is *not* classical.[9] Hancock moves out of the comping role he has inhabited since the beginning and ranges through strong right-handed melodic lines to two-fisted chords to cascades of running motives that pick up on the flourishes that he used to introduce and interrupt the tune. The solo is indeed elegant and graceful, but it is also quicksilver in its changes of ideas and infinitely resourceful, while maintaining artistic, intellectual, and expressive coherence. The two noticeable fluffs Hancock commits also help to remind us that we are experiencing the realm of vivid, fallible expression in the moment. Pat Metheny has spoken of the special quality of Herbie Hancock's playing: "Herbie, when he improvises, it's like you've heard it before. It gets to your human memory—to a place that you're remembering something that you didn't even know that you knew. He's got that sort of inevitable one-thing-follows-the-next, follows-the-next, follows-the-next thing that is so rare in modern improvisers."[10]

The elastic nature of the solos on this track is clearly illuminated by a perusal of Example 8. (The bass line has also been transcribed in Example 8 to help the reader keep track of the structure of the solo.) Hancock plays four choruses. His first chorus maps directly onto the twenty-two-measure format of the head. For the second chorus Hancock adds a four-measure interpolation before the four-measure VI-♭ii-V close (see measures 41–44 of Example 8). This bridges the D7♭5 to B♭maj7 progression of the original by moving from C to F. In the third chorus an *additional* four measures are added before the C to F interpolation (see measures 67–70), making a thirty-measure chorus. But for the fourth and last chorus of his solo, Hancock (as well as Carter and Williams, of course—they must have been forewarned about this accordionlike approach to the structure) not only omits these eight additional measures but also elides four measures of the original (corresponding to mm. 17–20 of the head), thus intensifying the ending and the entire final chorus.

Davis's return to a modified version of the melody he played at the opening readjusts the balance between tune and improvisation toward the head-solo-solo-solo-head conventional format. But his descending, sliding, falling-away, slowing-down ending is anything but conventional. As he stops, we hear him croak to the producer: "See how it sounds, Teo."

As in the other slow modal pieces mentioned, the role of the bass is crucial in establishing not only the beat (against the soft brushes of the drummer) but also the modal changes of the harmony. Carter plays with great subtlety on this track, constantly shifting his 3/4 patterns, or playing one note per measure on the pedal points, but favoring a quarter note/half note, high-low gesture that imparts lightness and lilt to the texture. Williams colors his line for each soloist, brushing exquisite waltz patterns on the snare for Davis, switching to sticks on the ride cymbal for Shorter (and adding patterns of even eighths, sixteenth/dotted eighth, and two against three), and moving from sticks to brushes

Example 8. Hancock solo on "Circle" from *Miles Smiles* (1966).

on the cymbals to brushes on the snare for Hancock. A beautiful effect is achieved at special moments by Williams falling completely silent. Percussionist Matthew Persing has expressively compared this effect to patches of canvas deliberately left uncovered in a painting.[11] One tom-tom hit signals Davis's return.

To complete the side, Macero placed "Footprints," another Wayne Shorter tune, next on the album. While "Circle" and "Orbits" were recorded (in that order) on October 24, 1966, "Footprints" and "Ginger Bread Boy" were recorded the next day. This is the longest track on the album, at 9 minutes and 44 seconds.[12] ("Orbits" and "Circle" are 4 minutes 35 seconds and 5 minutes and 52 seconds, respectively.) And its sense of spaciousness is

Example 9. Bass vamp on "Footprints" from *Miles Smiles* (1966).

immediately conveyed by an opening bass vamp (alone for two measures and then joined by piano and drums), which continues throughout the piece; by the meter, which is a broad 6/4; by the tempo (approximately dotted half note = 57); and by the mode, which is C Dorian (see Examples 9 and 10).[13] To confirm the C Dorian designation, note the A naturals in the opening measures of the melody. Note also how Carter's bass vamp omits the pitch A when the harmony shifts to F in measures 5 and 6—a pitch that would be expected at this point to continue the arpeggio pattern—in favor of playing B♭. This has two advantages: it provides a pattern of rising fourths: C-F-B♭-E♭, and it omits the A♭ pitch of the F-minor chord, which would contradict the modality of the harmony.

The pianist's addition of long, full modal chords in a broad interpretation of the meter and the drummer's wash of crosscurrents tapped out on cymbal complete the airy atmosphere against which Shorter's tune is projected. This is an original

Example 10. "Footprints" head from *Miles Smiles* (1966).

melody in three segments in a-a'-b or a-a'-a" form, contrasting a flat line with a descending one, whose first two segments end on the upbeat. The tune is in twelve measures, divided into three groups of four, the first group staying on the tonic, the second moving from iv to i, and the third from V to IV to i (see Example 11). If many of these features sound like those of the twelve-bar blues, it is no accident. The piece is cast very much as the blues, and the similarities to as well as differences from the conventional format are among its most intriguing aspects.

An inventory of the differences would include the meter and the mode, the bright harmonic clashes, especially in the last strain, and the continuous parallel fourths of the horns. The three phrases are beautifully balanced (see Example 10 again), sharing the opening gesture with its rhythmic kick into the second half of

```
i      i      i      i
iv     iv     i      i
V      IV     i      i
```

Example 11. "Footprints" head, harmonic layout.

the measure, but together they also stretch from incompletion to resolution. They do this in two ways. First literally: the first phrase is two measures long, the second and third three measures. But they also stretch rhetorically, with the first phrase ending abruptly on the upbeat before measure 3 and on a half cadence, and the second arching higher in the middle before echoing the half-cadence close in measure 7 (and thus sounding further along the spectrum of closure), while the last phrase finally hits the missing downbeat (slightly displaced) and the cadence to the tonic in measure 11.

I would also like to point out that circularity informs this, the third piece on the side, in addition to the other two. Shorter does not build in a dominant turnaround in the last measure of this blues. The harmony stays on C, thus linking the end and the beginning of each chorus seamlessly rather than through a V-I connection. This seamlessness is heightened by an important component of what the bassist plays.

In measures 9 and 10 of the form (the beginning of the final strain), the bassist double-times through the changes, precisely at the time when the harmonic progressions are occurring twice a measure instead of every two measures, in other words, four times as fast. The speed of the bass notes seems even faster than double time because of the rapidity of the chord changes and the disruption of the established pattern with its long note in the second half of each bar. (Indeed, the first time he plays it, the suddenness of this change causes Ron Carter to fall back from eighth notes to quarter notes earlier than planned. Thereafter, not only is he entirely secure but he also invents a different way of negotiating this passage each time it occurs.) Since the disruption of the pattern occurs in measures 9 and 10, and the bass returns to the vamp on C in measure 11, an ambiguity is created about the point of recommencement of the form, thus increasing the strength of the join. It is like a serpent holding its tail in its mouth.

Throughout the head (played twice) and during the two horn solos, the pianist takes a "responsive" role. He fills in gaps, waits for holes in the improvisations, matches the lyricism or intensity of the soloists, and either discreetly or aggressively but with great rhythmic ingenuity comps behind the players. His role in the head also serves to heighten the sense of blues structure: he plays always in the "empty measures" of the form, as instrumentalists have done since the invention of the blues.

Davis then takes a fiery solo built on eight choruses. The solo builds in intensity, and as always, Davis uses the length and brevity of his silences (which are colored by the ever-alert responses of Hancock and the waxing and waning accompaniment of Williams) as vital rhetorical elements of his playing. The solo is created from brief phrases, mostly rising, and from staccato bursts. There is no audible connection to the melodic makeup of the tune, and the sense of constant innovation is heightened by the lack of repetition and rare use of sequence. (There is a brief moment, from 3:28 to 3:42, when Davis worries the opening fragment of Ellington's "Rockin' in Rhythm.")[14] One of the only times he plays a descending sequence is just before the end, where the relative conventionality of the pattern acts as a sign of impending closure. In fact, Davis spills over his eight choruses by a couple of measures, leaving Shorter to enter on the second strain of the form, over the F section. However, Carter adapts immediately, turning Shorter's entrance into the beginning of the chorus and playing as though "from the top."

A further intriguing change in the music occurs in the middle of Davis's solo: everybody moves from 6/4 meter to 4/4.

Example 12. Diagram of 4/4 over 6/4 in bass vamp of "Footprints."

This does not happen all at once, and the shift is extremely subtle. The change is first signaled in the bass toward the end of Davis's second chorus, when, in the labile measures 9 and 10, Carter plays in four across the six. During the next chorus, Williams begins to emphasize beats one and four on the tomtom; by measures 9 and 10, the bass moves again to 4/4, and by the end of the chorus, everyone is playing in four. From this point on, until the return of the head at the end of the take, 4/4 is the prevailing meter. It should be emphasized that the 4/4 is laid directly over the 6/4, in other words, that a former dotted half note now exactly equals a half note (see Example 12). The bass vamp continues, and its feel is so similar that it would be easy to overlook the metrical shift.[15]

In his solo, Shorter alternates vivid, fast passages with more lyrical episodes. His five choruses depend somewhat more on sequential patterns than Davis's and have fewer silences. Hancock's accompaniment, in keeping with the different timbre of the solo instrument and the different feeling of the solo itself, is far more discreet, especially in the earlier choruses. Indeed, Hancock lays out for the first chorus. Shorter uses a different sign from that of Davis to signal closure. He quotes a melodic tag from the last phrase of the melody. This melodic tag can be heard in embryonic form at the end of Shorter's third chorus, as though he were trying it out. Even more fascinating is the following: Shorter also takes two extra measures after his four choruses, but as Hancock enters for his solo, Carter does *not* adapt. Is he aware from Hancock's chording that he knows exactly where he is? Are pianists better at thinking harmonically than horn players?

Hancock's solo is exclusively chordal, in keeping with the responses and fills he plays throughout the piece. In his second chorus he works at the old blues trick of phrase repetition over changing harmonies, building chords of aggressive Bartokian grit and playing them in jazz-rock rhythms. In the third chorus the blue notes in the chords turn to obsessive dissonance. This is the third piano solo on the album, and it is the third piano technique displayed, being chordal throughout. (The first was right hand only, the second a mixture of solo lines and chords.)

One of the special features of 6/4 meter is its multivalence. Tony Williams takes advantage of this feature to create endlessly varied permutations of twos and threes. His metrical and rhythmic creativity here is quite remarkable. Example 13 shows but a few of the ways Williams chooses to parse the meter, overlaying either fast or slow four-in-a-bar swing rhythms, or even quarters, or triplet quarters, or dotted quarters over the measures.

What this example cannot show is the way in which Williams, dividing the six quarters into eighths (or, in the 4/4 section, the four quarters into triplets), nudges them with delicate flexibility back and forth along the spectrum between straight and swung and, like a choosy royal picking out precious stones, puts his emphasis on now one, now another among any one of these twelve notes. This is accomplished almost exclusively on cymbals, switching among them and among places of contact, so that the wash of color is constantly changing. At places of particular significance (end of a solo, beginning of a new solo) or places that he makes significant (urging a soloist to intensity), he mixes in syncopated (snareless) snare or tom-tom hits or cymbal crashes.

Example 13. Some of the metric permutations played by Tony Williams on "Footprints."

A subtle tension is created throughout the piece by the obstinate nature of the bass vamp. Its continued presence provides a rigid framework for the fantasies of all the solos.

The return of the head (after one slightly robbed and two full choruses by Hancock) is signaled by a return to lighter comping by Hancock and a slowing down of note values at the quick-change measures by both Carter and Williams (with Williams even fading out for a full beat at the end of the chorus). But the circularity of the tune and the spontaneity of the event make for an indecisive ending. The indecision is made more palpable by the fact that the horns, in returning, as it were, to the opening, try to play the 6/4 tune over the now established 4/4 accompaniment. The momentary awkwardness can be heard quite clearly. Williams is not ready to stop after twice more through the head, and he initiates another repeat. As the rhythm section ploughs ahead, Hancock leaves Williams to take a solo over Carter's vamp. Again the horns play the head. Again the bass and drums continue (with Carter trying a phrase or two in 5/4!), until they slow down and find a stopping place. Another quiet "Hey, Teo" is left in at the very end of the track. (In the 1992 reissue, produced by John Snyder for Sony/Columbia, there are nine extra seconds on this track that were not included on the original LP or on the 1998 boxed set,[16] during which Davis continues, "You can take *any* part of that you want," and someone else adds, laughing, "And throw it or put it in the trash!")

But in this rather scrappy ending, it is the unspoken messages that seem to be particularly thick in the air: Davis pulling Shorter in for the extra repeats, Hancock handing over to Williams, Carter and Williams signaling to each other throughout. Most revealing in the context of this powerfully interactive group are those messages that are audibly ignored or overridden. Three times Davis signals an ending (at the "right" place after twice through the head and at the end of both "extra" repeats), either by slowing down on the three eighths at the end of measure 10, or by elongating his final pitch, or by effecting a fade, apparently by backing away from the microphone. In all three cases, one or another of the members of the rhythm section carries on regardless. First Williams urges the music on. After the first "extra" head, Carter switches to a slow four, immediately joined by Williams, apparently in readiness for a close, but this time Hancock opens up as though for an extra solo. However, Williams decides he wants to get some solo time in, signaling this by playing short rolls and moving rapidly from tom-toms to cymbals to snare. Hancock leaves him the stage. Williams plays some solo licks over a steady bass pattern (Carter returns to 6/4 and remains on his C arpeggio throughout). When Williams is finished, he signals the horns by returning to the quick high hat pattern he had played throughout the performance. Horns and piano play one more "extra" repeat, the end of which is again ignored by Carter and Williams, but the horns are done, and drum and bass peter to an end. It is all this additional business, stretching the take from 7 minutes and 58 seconds to 9 minutes and 42 seconds (an extra one and three-quarter minutes, nearly two minutes including the banter), that presumably occasioned the "throw-away" comments and amusement at the end. (For a schematic representation of all the events in "Footprints" and their durations, see Figure 2 on pp. 76–77.) But the kind of give-and-take in evidence in these last extra minutes is emblematic of the magical interplay among these five gifted musicians and must have been the primary reason for the producer's decision to leave them in. Teo Macero, who has produced some 3,000 records in his career so far and does not have a very detailed recollection of the sessions for this particular one, says now that he kept all this material and Davis's comments at the end of the other tracks on the album "for fun." According to Macero, Davis left all editing decisions to him. (Macero: "He never came to the editing room, except maybe four or five times in the twenty-nine or thirty years I was associated with him." JY: "Did he ever have any suggestions?" Macero: "No." JY: "Never?" Macero: "Not in all the years I was with him.")[17]

It is extremely revealing to compare this performance of "Footprints" with the one on Wayne Shorter's own album *Adam's Apple*, recorded about eight months earlier.[18] On this album Shorter plays with Herbie Hancock, Reginald Workman on bass, and Joe Chambers on drums. The first difference one notices is the tempo. Shorter originally recorded this piece at a more leisurely pace (approximately dotted half note=44, compared with Davis's tempo of approximately dotted half note = 57). Davis's tempo gives the performance a little more urgency. Second, Shorter's first recording has only one horn. The duet of Davis and Shorter playing the head in parallel fourths on *Miles Smiles* adds significantly to the modal, nontraditional quality of the performance. Third, on Shorter's original recording the accompaniment and the three solos (sax, piano, bass) are much more conventional. The bassist drops the vamp once the solos start, only returning to it at the end of his solo to signal the return of the head, and the drummer plays a waltz shuffle on his ride cymbal through almost the entire piece. Davis's decision to continue the vamp throughout, the tension this provides, and the freedom it gives *his* drummer are vital components of his new vision for the music. The players on the original version stick to the original 6/4 meter throughout, whereas Davis has the meter shift in the middle of his recording. Davis has reworked an already interesting composition into something more intense, freer, and more sophisticated. As for the solos on the original recording, Shorter stays recognizably close to the melody during his improvisation. Hancock has some interesting ideas, but his solo contains patterns of lengthy sequential playing, and the bassist is, well, workmanlike.

A comparison of the Shorter solos on these two recordings provides considerable insight not only into the ways Shorter's own playing was influenced by his joining the Davis quintet but also into the differences in musical style between that of a bop band and the new post-bop music created by Miles Davis. Let us look first at Shorter's solo from "Footprints" on *Adam's Apple*, recorded in February 1966 (see Example 14).

The first observation to make is that this is an excellent solo. Shorter takes four choruses, building his solo by moving from close to the tune to further from it, from spacious to more crammed, from mostly quarters and eighths to many sixteenths,

Example 14. Wayne Shorter's solo from "Footprints" on *Adam's Apple*.

and from mid- and high range to altissimo. He creates tuneful ideas from swung eighths and triplet patterns, and some of these ideas are shared among choruses. With the exception of the boundary between third and fourth chorus, he beautifully anticipates the new focus of each chorus a measure or two early, thereby simultaneously creating cohesion and covering the joins in the form. This is particularly noticeable at the end of the second chorus. However, the bones of the tune are clearly palpable beneath the skin of the solo. In every chorus there are phrases from the tune (see measures 6, 7, 9, 10, 18, 19, 21, 34, 45, and 46), and these phrases occur at the same place in the chorus as they do in the tune. Harmonically the solo is relatively conservative, with the chord changes plainly audible, especially at the dominant harmony (see measures 9, 21, 33, and 45).

Shorter's solo on "Footprints" from *Miles Smiles* (remember this was recorded only eight months after the sessions for *Adam's Apple*) is different (see Example 15). It is far more abstract, with a less clearly defined trajectory from beginning to end and with fewer ties to the head; it is also in 4/4 instead of 6/4. He devises rhythmic and melodic patterns across the tune and across the form. The phrases are more disjunctive, more various, and with more spaces than in the earlier solo. The harmony is further "out," and each chorus is less individually cohesive. His five choruses refer to the melody only twice, in measures 33 and 57, both times at the dominant harmony.[19] His approach to soloing is clearly influenced by Davis, whose solo precedes his (as always on this recording) and is lengthy (eight choruses), highly intense (often high on open horn), inventive, epigrammatic, and without reference to the melodic components of the tune. It goes without saying that the effect of both horn solos is deeply colored by their powerfully active and interactive context, made up of strong modal comping on the piano, constantly varied coloring from the drums and cymbals, and the curiously hypnotic quality of the bass, which projects overall stasis with regular introjections of exuberance (at the ninth and tenth measure of each chorus).

Finally I would like to point out one small but crucial difference in the head of these two tunes. Davis has changed Shorter's original melody (see Example 16 and compare with Example 10). On *Adam's Apple*, Shorter fills in the "empty" measures of the melody (measures 3, 4, and 8) with echoes of the last two notes (pitches D–C, the closing gesture) of the first and second phrase. In fact, the second time through the head (he plays the head twice, both at the beginning and end of the performance), he adds a rather self-conscious trill to the Ds.

Example 15. Wayne Shorter's solo on "Footprints" from *Miles Smiles*.

Example 16. Wayne Shorter's original version of "Footprints" from *Adam's Apple*.

It is a superb indicator of Davis's incisive new thinking that he decided to omit these echoes. Not only do the omissions allow the phrases to build additively in the way I have described above, but they also create spaces in the melody—spaces that give room for Hancock's modal chording in the head and that generate the intensely expressive silences that are such a vital component of Davis's own solo in his reworking of this haunting new blues.

10. The Album *Miles Smiles*, Side 2

The second side of the album (in its original LP format) contains three up-tempo numbers: Shorter's "Dolores" and the two tunes by composers outside the group: "Freedom Jazz Dance" and "Ginger Bread Boy." "Dolores" is another example, like "Footprints," of Shorter's ability to create something riveting out of a very small amount of material. Chambers describes the material as a "catch-phrase" and suggests insightfully that "the quality that distinguishes both ["Footprints" and "Dolores"] is the clarity of the mood that the catch-phrase . . . encodes."[1]

The mood of "Dolores" is perky and quirky. The tempo is very fast (approximately quarter note=278 beats per minute), short melodic statements are followed by gaps filled only by bass and drums, the harmonic path is erratic, and the form is palindromic (see Example 17).

The overall form of the head can be represented as ABCBA. A stands for an eight-bar phrase for the horns, B for a matching

Example 17. "Dolores" head from *Miles Smiles* (1966).

passage for bass and drums alone, and C for a six-bar phrase in the middle.

A	8 mm.	Horns (with bass and drums)
B	8 mm.	Bass and drums only
C	6 mm.	Horns (with bass and drums)
B	8 mm.	Bass and drums only
A	8 mm.	Horns (with bass and drums)

But this simple outline obscures both variants and similarities among the components of this composition. First, there are subtle but significant changes in the first three measures of the "return" of the A section. Second, the bass and drum passages labeled B move in different directions. Finally, the C section is actually based on the same rhythmic sequence (and a partial melodic inversion) of the A phrase.

This highly original tune wonderfully combines feelings of oddity, cliché, easygoing freedom, and slight obsession. Its oddity comes from the asymmetry of the phrasing and the stop-and-go construction, its sense of cliché and insouciance from the melodic profile and rhythmic push to the downbeat, and its obsessive quality from the constant rhythmic sequences, the similarity (or near identity) of the melodic components, and the stopping and restarting of the horns.

While the opening melody appears symmetrical as a result of its overall eight-bar shape, the phrasing within those eight bars is not symmetrical at all. The first phrase is two and a half measures long, its continuation two measures long, and its consequent two measures extended by one and a half. (I have labeled these phrases in Example 17.) The middle part (or C section) of the head is cleverly different and similar. It begins with an unexpected pickup and continues with modified intervals and inversions, although its rhythmic profile is clearly an echo of the opening section. This sets up an expectation that is not fulfilled, since what I have called the consequent phrase is suppressed and the phrase ends early, cut short both literally and in its rhetoric at six measures and on the last (staccato) eighth note of the measure. The final section is mostly a repetition of the first but with a little interval tampering and inversions of its own in the opening two and a half measures. The harmony of the first section moves from D minor to D♭ major mostly by whole and half steps. The middle section contains some dominant-tonic movement, giving it the harmonic *feel* of a bridge.

The opening of the head is played at first by Shorter alone, and Davis joins him in unison for the second and third melodic statements. Williams surrounds the head largely with a wash of cymbals only, thus putting greater focus on the bass, especially during the B sections, in which Carter plays alone with Williams. Once again there is no piano comping on this track. Carter indulges in some fancy leaps, double stopping, and long glissandos during his two eight-bar spots, though when he is walking the (very fast) fours, his sound is, as always, both fat and buoyant.

Williams and Carter manage to provide a background for the solos that is provocative, pushing, solid, and free. Williams splashes and lashes with irregular comments underneath a chattering cymbal. He moves all over the drum set, swinging hard, right on the edge of the beat, but without any predictable pattern, and supplying swaths and patches of color. Carter is mostly walking, although the walking is constantly new, constantly changing direction, and often interspersed with more double stops and crossing meters.

The solos hew to the eight-bar patterns, eschewing the six-measure phrase. Davis is particularly garrulous in his solo, with very few of his usual pregnant pauses or screaming silences. He bases his improvisation on irregular mountains of eighth notes, incorporating occasional theme fragments from the head. The only time there is a significant gap is immediately before he plays a brief quotation about fifteen seconds before the end of his

Example 18. Quotation played by Miles Davis on "Dolores" at 1:37.

solo, at 1:37 (see Example 18). One can almost hear him latching on to the quotation as the figure he is manipulating brings it before his consciousness.[2]

Shorter's solo is almost exactly the same length as Davis's, although he creates a kaleidoscope of constantly changing figures as contrasted with Davis's longer lines. He too utilizes fragments of the tune, but he takes flight from them, manipulates them, distorts them, as opposed to embedding them in his solo. Shorter was asked about this solo and about the overall approach of the band at this point in their work during his 2000 interview for *Jazz Improv*. His answer is revealing. The interviewer says:

> We have a transcription of "Dolores" from the *Miles Smiles* album. When you were with Miles, what was the structure or basis for improvisation by individual group members on that composition? On the tune itself, the melody is quite clear and the changes are clear, but as I listen to the improvised section, I'm unclear as to whether there was a specific direction for people to follow. Could you discuss that a little bit?

Shorter answers:

> I think what happened there, I'm pretty sure, is that everyone who played, after the melody and all of that stuff, took a portion of a certain characteristic of the song, and—you can stay there. And then you do eight measures of it, and then you make your own harmonic road or avenue within a certain eight measures. But not counting out the eight measures, it's like whatever you fancied. But you keep the flavor. It was keeping the flavor of "Dolores" without—in other words, now as I look back—we were actually tampering with something called DNA in music in a song. Each song has its DNA.

So you just do the DNA and not the whole song. You do the characteristics. You say, "Okay, I will do the ear of the face, I will do the left side of the face. You do the right side of the face."[3]

Hancock makes no reference to the theme but begins his solo with a nod to the descending figure that Shorter had ended with. Hancock once again plays only with his right hand and this time stays mostly in the middle range of the instrument, using intense running eighth-note figures of irregular length and shape, breaking out into more varied note lengths toward the end of his solo. He plays longer than either of the others (about 1 minute and 40 seconds as opposed to about 1 minute and 15 seconds) and ignores an obvious cue from Williams to draw to a close. The ingenuity of his playing certainly justifies his decision.

The horns come back in on the six-measure phrase that had been ignored during the solos. Like the ending of "Footprints," the ending of "Dolores" is scrappy. Nobody seems to know when to end, and Davis and Shorter tease each other by starting and stopping the "final" run through the theme (last eight-measure phrase) several times. Once they get together, they play it six times. At the end of the third time, Hancock contributes a big two-fisted chord (the only chord in the piece) as though to signal an ending. But this is ignored, and Davis does the signaling by playing louder and more deliberately the last (sixth) time. But even this is not the end. Davis rips off a brief rising figure, as though to begin a new solo. But he leaves Williams to end the piece with several flourishes. On the 1992 reissue, you can hear Davis say hoarsely to his producer: "Teo, we played the ending about *six* times!"

Eddie Harris's "Freedom Jazz Dance" (the second track on Side 2) had been recorded by Harris (tenor sax), Ray Codrington (trumpet), Cedar Walton (piano), and Ron Carter (bass), with Billy Higgins on drums, in August 1965.[4] It is a funky piece, with a bluesy piano vamp, a bouncing bass line, and regularly syncopated drums, in the spirit of Herbie Hancock's "Watermelon Man" and "Cantaloupe Island," although the melodic line itself is made up almost entirely of leaping eighth notes, wandering (somewhat chromatically) over, around, and through a B♭7 (or B♭-diminished) chord, and ending with a high punch.

Once again, Miles Davis transforms the original.[5] First he takes the tune quite a bit faster (approximately quarter note = 194 instead of 166). Then he separates out the three phrases of the tune by inserting two measures of rest after the first and second phrases and four measures of rest after the third. Finally, he eliminates the funk vamp by taking out the piano (which now plays single big chords at the end of each phrase);[6] by having the bass play freely (although it retains the B♭ pedal); and by asking the drummer to chatter away continuously on snare triplets and high hat. (See Example 19.)

The cumulative effect of these changes is to make the piece more driving and considerably more abstract. Gone are the foot-tapping, dance-oriented, bluesy, repetitive sounds of funk, and in their place is a serious piece of abstract music making.[7]

Tony Williams plays particularly imaginatively on this track. He snaps the high hat on every beat, leaving his hands free for rolls of irregular length, cymbal splashes, and cross rhythms.[8] He changes color and feel for each soloist, while the constant light triplets on cymbal and snare add strongly to the overall sense of delicate intensity. Carter invents endless ways of directing his phrases, constructed mostly in two-measure lines to match the newly chiseled opening, down to the B♭ pedal.

After four finger snaps and a brief false start, the band plays twice through the head (trumpet and sax in unison). On the third phrase, Davis joins in a measure and a half late, an error (?) he repeats the second time through, perhaps to make it sound deliberate. (He does the same thing on the head at the end, compounding the suspicion that it might have been a deliberately

Example 19. "Freedom Jazz Dance" head from *Miles Smiles* (1966), indicating gaps inserted by Davis.

delayed entry. There is no doubt, however, that the first time it *sounds* like a mistake.)

Davis's solo is a model of his newly abstract style (see Example 20). He plays mostly in the middle range,[9] using brief scalar patterns, repeated notes, and short irregular phrases, but the lapidary solo makes constant reference to the tune by means of significant melodic fragments.[10] Davis manipulates the elements of the tune in a masterly manner. For instance, recognizing that the tune's cell structure is a two-eighth-note pattern, he suspends two-eighth-note motives in the background wash of bass, drums, and sparse comping chords. He also dissects the tune into eighth-note patterns, or spreads out its components, or isolates the final punching note. (In Example 20, the eighth-note motif and its variants are marked with an *x*, and melodic fragments of the tune are indicated with an *m*.) Since the harmony is so stable, Davis is faced with the challenge of playing both into

Example 20. Davis solo on "Freedom Jazz Dance" from *Miles Smiles* (1966).

and out of the pedal harmony. This problem he resolves in a remarkably musical and intelligent way, creating a balance between phrases centered on various versions of B♭ and those suggesting other harmonies, or outlining diminished chords, or creating patterns in fourths.

As always, Davis uses silence to great effect. The statistics are revealing. Out of 87 measures of this solo, the rests add up to about 38 measures, or about 44 percent. More revealing, of course, is a consideration of how, where, and why Davis uses silence. In general, he was a master of understatement and obliqueness, and saying less was his rhetorical method. Individual short phrases gain in meaning when they are isolated, and here every phrase counts, even those of two eighth notes. (In this case, the isolation of the phrases echoes Davis's "compositional" separation of the tune's originally crammed statements.) The silences create expectation and tension. The two-eighth-note motif may occur by itself, or it may be expanded into a longer phrase. It may appear at the beginning or the end of a measure, and it may or may not have a pickup. A melodic phrase may be a fragment of the tune, or it may be newly created. The silences allow these questions to remain in play throughout the solo.

Shorter's solo is even more abstract than that of Davis. He rarely refers to the tune, instead creating little winding phrases that are gradually aggregated as the solo proceeds. His tessitura is much wider than Davis's, covering most of the instrument. His solo increases in intensity as it proceeds, and Hancock facilitates this by beginning to comp much more actively and rhythmically about halfway through. Williams also becomes busier and more active.

Shorter's solo is followed by both horns playing the first segment of the theme, as though they had forgotten the pianist. Somehow the signal is communicated that Hancock does indeed want to take a solo, and he comes in after four measures. The focus is mostly on the right hand, although he comps lightly for himself with the left, and both hands join for occasional chords or sequential gestures in octaves. His melodic phrases are tinged by a new color, the Mixolydian mode on B♭. Hancock's solo is cut short by Davis reprising the head, soon joined by Shorter, and after twice through, the rhythm section ends the piece as it began. Impressions of Davis's focus, Shorter's relative garrulousness, and Hancock's brevity are confirmed by the actual length of the solos: Davis 1 minute and 46 seconds, Shorter 2 minutes and 10 seconds, Hancock 1 minute and 20 seconds (see Figure 2 on pp. 76–77).

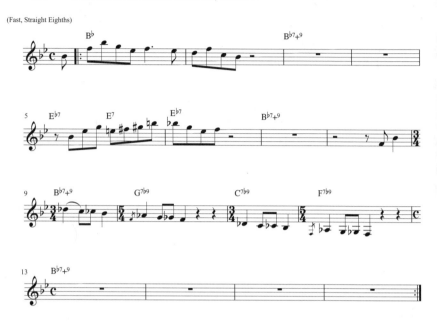

Example 21. "Ginger Bread Boy" head, as recorded by Jimmy Heath (1964).

The last tune on the record is another borrowed item, this time from Davis's (brief) onetime band member, Jimmy Heath. The middle of the three Heath brothers, Jimmy played alto, tenor, and flute and composed and arranged. Davis had recorded one of his pieces, "CTA," in 1953 on his album *Young Man with a Horn*.[11]

"Ginger Bread Boy" is the most fiery and, at approximately quarter note=284, the fastest track on *Miles Smiles*.[12] Again, Davis transforms the original. Heath had recorded this tune on his album *On the Trail* for Riverside in the spring of 1964 (see Example 21).[13] He was accompanied by Kenny Burrell (guitar), Wynton Kelly (piano), Paul Chambers (bass), and Albert Heath (drums). They play the tune at about quarter note=226, which is fast but comfortable. The group sound is relatively light, since the "second horn" is a guitar. And the solos are clean, precise, and conservatively chord-based, with the underlying progressions

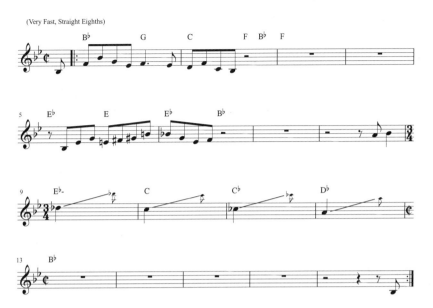

Example 22. "Ginger Bread Boy" head, as recorded by the Miles Davis Quintet (1966).

clearly reflected in the trajectory of the solos and the structural joins reassuringly acknowledged.

Davis takes the tune at a tempo that is almost manic. He plays it nearly 30 percent faster than Heath. He exaggerates the terse, epigrammatic nature of the original by introducing what Bob Belden has called the "stop-and-go concept" played by bass and drums in the interstices of the tune (see Example 22).[14] Carter, who provides the main timekeeping element on this record, plays two notes and then stops in measures 3 and 4 and 7 and 8, while Williams is especially active. The piece deliberately suggests the blues, being based on I (B♭) for the first four measures, moving to IV (E♭) for measures 5 and 6, and returning to B♭ for measures 7 and 8. Thenceforth the music, as originally conceived by Heath (see Example 21 again), expands to fill a sixteen-bar form, introducing a shifting meter (3/4, 5/4, 3/4, 5/4) in measures 9–12 and returning to the tonic via a circle-of-fifths progression (G7♭9-C7♭9-F7♭9-B♭7+9). Davis, however, rewrites the melody at measures 9–12, substituting four upward-smearing gestures for the sequential descending phrases of the original (see Example 22). He also intensifies the metrical shift at this point, replacing Heath's 3/4 plus 5/4 combinations, which fall happily into eight-beat totals, with four 3/4 measures, which are more disruptive. Not surprisingly, these gestures become the most memorable features of the performance. After this, Davis places five measures for bass and drums, which round out the sixteen-measure form.

The most prolific player on this track is undoubtedly Tony Williams. He is enormously active, producing an endless, constantly varied stream of rhythms and colors. In particular one hears washes of sound, such as those he creates on high hat, ride cymbal, and soft snare. In an interview in 1995, Hancock described Williams as "a phenomenon. Nobody was playing like him. He was creating a whole new approach to drumming. . . . Tony was one of the strongest elements in that band. [There was] a lot of responsibility on the drums to give the band a certain fiery, dynamic personality."[15]

Fiery and *dynamic* are certainly words to describe Williams's playing on "Ginger Bread Boy." He manages to combine great freedom with an extremely intense rhythmic drive. Principal rhythmic significance is provided by the bassist, however, who can suggest a sense of continuity or stasis simply through his note choices. It is he who is responsible for making the music "stop" in measures 3–4 and 7–8 and "go" again in measures 13–16. And the clarity, variety, solidity, and urgency of his playing throughout are remarkable. He also plays differently under each soloist, ranging freely through the rhythms for the first part of Davis's and Hancock's solos before settling into walking patterns; walking half notes and ranging higher as Shorter builds the intensity of his solo; and then dropping in volume

Example 23. Quotation played by Herbie Hancock
on "Ginger Bread Boy" at 6:23.

and range when Hancock enters. Williams also increases in volume and activity through Shorter's solo and drops down immediately after Hancock enters. But Hancock also builds up his solo from tentative to fluent, from short statements to much longer ones, and from midrange to high on the keyboard. At 6:23 Hancock lets slip a tiny quotation, which may possibly be from "Turkey in the Straw" but probably isn't (see Example 23).[16] Throughout the solo, Carter and Williams simultaneously follow the trajectory of his musical impulse and urge him on. All three soloists take eight choruses, although the relationship of these solos to the underlying chordal structure is very free. Once again melodic fragments are embedded in wide-ranging and newly devised patterns, especially in Shorter's solo, which makes frequent reference to the upward thrusts of the 3/4 measures in Davis's adaptation of the tune. It is perhaps appropriate that at the end of the piece Carter and Williams play alone for an extra thirty seconds, making brief forays into new areas, and again both stretching and relaxing the forward momentum before bringing the track to a close.

These last two tracks on *Miles Smiles* indicate perhaps more clearly than anything else how Miles Davis had regained his creative power and energy since the somewhat uncertain early years of the 1960s. A comparison of "Freedom Jazz Dance" and "Ginger Bread Boy" with their original recordings, fourteen months and two and a half years earlier, respectively, also shows how far he had traveled from the perfectly capable, skilled work of his contemporaries. All these performances, in October 1966, are radical reinventions of jazz style, from bop and hard bop, with their satisfying, somewhat predictable, always solidly grounded approach, to a dangerous, high-flying, exhilarating act of communal communication, virtuosity, and trust. Davis brought together on one album "free" playing and chord-based improvisation, rhythmic innovation and timekeeping, elastic form and rigid structure, "modal" music and chord changes. He introduced a new sound for a conventional instrument, having the piano enter, right hand only, for "horn" solos, and he significantly altered the traditional roles of bass and drums. His vision in doing all this cannot be overstated, nor can the importance of the extraordinary skill and musicianship of every other member of his band.[17]

But perhaps these achievements also owed something to another musician who was no longer in Davis's band—a musician whose presence Davis had missed painfully until he found Wayne Shorter—a musician whose activities he must have followed closely during these years: John Coltrane. Coltrane played like "five tenor players," according to Davis. But more significant for Davis's stylistic development, in my view, was the fact that Coltrane had started his own band after leaving Davis and that this band, once established, played and stayed together from the end of 1961 until the fall of 1965 and was highly successful precisely during those years when Davis was floundering.[18] This was also a remarkable band and highly interactive, made up of brilliant individuals, with an innovative piano player, McCoy Tyner, a rock-solid but creative bassist, Jimmy Garrison, and an extremely powerful drummer, Elvin Jones.[19] Jones has described the quartet of those years: "It felt like a perfect blend, a joy. It was always a joy to play, in a recording studio or a nightclub. It was the same feeling, in front of a large audience or no one at all. Music was our sole purpose."[20]

I have suggested in chapter 7 that Davis's recording of "Someday My Prince Will Come" was influenced by Coltrane's "My Favorite Things."[21] But Coltrane's influence on Davis in the early 1960s was deeper and stronger than that. From December

1961 to September 1965, Coltrane's group made many recordings at Rudy Van Gelder's studio in New Jersey, resulting in an
output of six major albums (others were released after his death):
Coltrane, Ballads, Impressions, Crescent, A Love Supreme, and *The
John Coltrane Quartet Plays.*[22] Davis could not and did not want to
follow Coltrane down every trail he blazed: he avoided the reli-
giosity, the streams of notes. And indeed, it is significant that
Coltrane's band was a quartet, while Davis always favored a
quintet. Where Coltrane was garrulous, Davis was terse; where
Coltrane seemed to indulge in excess and overstatement, Davis's
rhetorical modes were concision and ellipsis.[23] Coltrane was a
virtuoso; Davis was a trumpet player whose urge to express
himself often seemed a struggle to overcome his own limitations
and those of his instrument.[24] Davis always needed a foil. But
despite these differences, in the first half of the 1960s the one
band that might have stood as a model (as well as a challenge)
for Miles Davis was that of John Coltrane. In 1965 Coltrane won
Jazzman of the Year, Record of the Year (*A Love Supreme*), and
first place in the *Down Beat* tenor saxophone poll.[25] And in his biography of Davis, Quincy Troupe reports that in the mid-1980s
the only photographs Davis displayed in his home (and that he
carried with him every time he moved between his apartment in
New York and his house in Malibu) were those of Gil Evans and
John Coltrane.[26]

Conclusion: Miles Does Smile

In the first half of the 1960s, Davis was in a slump. He had been assaulted by a policeman. He was in physical pain, drinking too much, and using cocaine. His father and mother died within two years of each other. His wife left him. Audiences were turning to rock music. Jazz clubs were closing. But worst of all, "the music wasn't happening." He had no band, and the man he most enjoyed playing with had become successful without him.

In 1949 Davis had begun to create a personal approach both to playing and to conceiving music. His new conception led to the formation of a new jazz style, named cool. By the mid-1950s he had forged an individual and distinctive sound and was "orchestrating" the music of his combos in new and compelling ways. His innovative thinking led again to new musical styles, including hard bop and his special muted introspective ballads. He also found individuals with whom he could create his performances live and on record. In 1958 and 1959 he led a sextet whose work culminated in the transcendent *Kind of Blue* and the invention of yet another approach to the music (modal). Then his world began to fall apart.

Davis's renaissance in the mid-1960s was catalyzed by his finding younger players whose dedication, open-mindedness, and extraordinary musical skills reanimated his own.[1] He regained his creative energy and thought his way through to a new approach to the music, an approach that was abstract and intense in the extreme, with space created for the rhythmic and coloristic independence of the drummer—an approach that incorporated modal and chordal harmonies, flexible form, structured choruses, melodic variation, and free improvisation. It was freedom anchored in form. We can call it post bop.

In the second half of the 1960s Davis had once again put together a group whose members communicated deeply with each other and simultaneously with their audiences. Together these men made music that was fiery, new, contemplative, and challenging. It was music that perfectly balanced structure and freedom, the individual and the group, innovation and tradition. We can hear this magic in the recordings from that time, and we can hear it especially in the remarkable *Miles Smiles*, recorded in October 1966 and released in 1967.

By January 1968, less than fifteen months after the recording sessions for *Miles Smiles*, Davis was already searching for something new. He experimented by adding guitarists to the group (Joe Beck, George Benson, and Bucky Pizzarelli), having Hancock play on electric piano, and working toward the bass-groove, rock-influenced sound that characterized his music from the late 1960s until 1975.[2] But for the acoustic, interactive, intense music-making period of the mid-1960s, *Miles Smiles* was a highpoint. No wonder Miles was smiling.

Notes

Introduction

1. These are described throughout his autobiography. See Miles Davis with Quincy Troupe, *Miles: The Autobiography* (New York: Simon and Schuster, 1989), 14–15, 72, 83, 128–29, 163, 169, 194, 231, 271, 306–307, 325, 334, 361–62, 405.

2. "A vague term," *New Grove Dictionary of Jazz,* 2nd ed. (London: Macmillan, 2002); "The period from the mid 1950's until the mid 1960's represent[ing] the heyday of mainstream modern jazz," *Marc Sabatella's Jazz Improvisation Primer,* http://www.outsideshore.com/primer/primer/ms-primer-2-6.html; "Post bop is a collective term for mainstream jazz styles that developed from bebop, cool jazz, and hard bop, but which add other elements as well," *Jazz Styles: Mainstream Jazz: Post Bop,* http://www.outsideshore.com/school/music/almanac/html/Jazz_Styles/Mainstream_Jazz/Post_Bop.htm; "Also referred to as hard bop, this form took the rhythms, ensemble structure, and energy of bebop and combined the added horn, similar playlists, and continued to use Latin elements," John Ephland, "*Down Beat's* Jazz 101," http://www.downbeat.com/default.asp?sect=education&subsect=jazz_15; "Post-bop can refer to a variety of Jazz music that is post-bebop chronologically," Gerard Cox, "Building a Jazz Library: Post-Bop Records of the Modern Era," http://www.allaboutjazz.com/library/postbop.htm.

1. Miles Smiles?

1. The apparent incongruity of Miles smiling has been noted in the Austrian jazz journal *JazzLive* 13 (1984) by Rainer Rygalyk in an article entitled "Miles Never Smiles" as well as in the liner notes to the original album (Columbia CL 2601/CS 9401), where Anthony Tuttle writes: "Miles smiles? Wow! What have we here? Who's kidding

who? . . . Miles *smiles*? . . . Is someone putting us on?" In his somewhat self-serving "biography" of Davis, *Miles and Me* (Berkeley: University of California Press, 2000), Quincy Troupe describes how Davis hated being photographed with a smile. "Miles could be very gentle, loving and funny, and he smiled a lot. It was just that he didn't want the public to see that side of him" (94).

2. Jack Chambers, *Milestones: The Music and Times of Miles Davis*, 2 vols. (Toronto: University of Toronto Press, 1989; reprint, New York: Da Capo, 1998), 1:89, 94.

3. Davis, *Autobiography*, 297.

4. In his personal style Davis was also influenced by Jimi Hendrix. See Charley Gerard, *Jazz in Black and White: Race, Culture, and Identity in the Jazz Community* (Westport, Conn.: Praeger, 1998), 120.

5. Arnold Shaw, *52nd St.: The Street of Jazz* (New York: Da Capo, 1977), ix–xiv; John Edward Hasse, *Beyond Category: The Life and Genius of Duke Ellington* (New York: Da Capo, 1995), 295, 309.

6. "Birdland History," http://www.birdlandjazz.com/history.html; *New Grove Jazz*, s.v. "Nightclubs and Other Venues: USA, New York, Birdland."

7. For a highly politicized and jargon-filled discussion of the "blackness" of jazz, see Herman Gray, "Jazz Tradition, Institutional Formation, and Cultural Practice: The Canon and the Street as Frameworks for Oppositional Black Cultural Politics," in *From Sociology to Cultural Studies: New Perspectives*, ed. Elizabeth Long (Malden, Mass.: Blackwell, 1997), 351–73.

8. Quincy Troupe reports that "Gil Evans was Miles' best friend, bar none." See Troupe, *Miles and Me*, 70.

9. Interview conducted with Teo Macero, March 31, 2000. Macero has also quoted Davis using "marriage" to describe their relationship. See Antoni Roszczuk, "Teo Macero: 'A Producer Must Encourage the Artist to Do New Things,' " *Jazz Forum: The Magazine of the International Jazz Federation* 50 (1977): 39.

10. In addition to the music contained on those six albums—*E.S.P.* (Columbia CS 9150, issued 1965), *Miles Smiles* (Columbia CS 9401, issued 1967), *Sorcerer* (Columbia CS 9532, issued 1967), *Nefertiti* (Columbia CS 9594, issued 1968), *Miles in the Sky* (Columbia CS 9628, issued

1968), and *Filles de Kilimanjaro* (Columbia CS 34396, issued 1969)—other tracks recorded at this time were held back and only released later, on *Water Babies* (Columbia C 34396, 1976), *Circle in the Round* (Columbia KC2 36278, 1979), and *Directions* (Columbia KC2 36474, 1981).

11. Chambers, *Milestones*, 1:78.

12. Todd Coolman, liner notes to *Miles Davis Quintet, 1965–68* (Columbia 4-67398).

13. Eric Nisenson, *'Round About Midnight: A Portrait of Miles Davis* (New York: Dial, 1982), 196.

14. Harvey Pekar, "Miles Davis: 1964–69 Recordings," *Coda* (1976): 8–14; reprinted in *A Miles Davis Reader*, ed. Bill Kirchner (Washington, D.C.: Smithsonian Institution Press, 1997), 164–83.

15. Kirchner, ed., *A Miles Davis Reader*, 164. Ted Gioia, *The History of Jazz* (New York: Oxford University Press, 1997) describes *E.S.P., Miles Smiles*, and *Nefertiti* as "classic recordings" (332). Richard Cook, *It's About That Time: Miles Davis On and Off Record* (New York: Oxford University Press, 2007), calls *Miles Smiles* "one of the most satisfying documents by this edition of the quintet" (175). Views such as these are not universally held. Of *Miles Smiles*, John Litweiler wrote, "[T]here's no denying that the level of energy and adventure has slipped. . . . [A]mbiguity is not the same as the simple vagueness of [Herbie Hancock's] wilted solo melodies and sequences. . . . Bassist Ron Carter plays facile lines . . . he also tends to sound jaded." See John Litweiler, *The Freedom Principle: Jazz after 1958* (New York: William Morrow, 1984), 125–26.

16. Louis-Victor Mialy, "Ron Carter: Un géant des profondeurs," *Jazz Hot*, May 1983, 400.

17. Herbie Hancock, quoted by Todd Coolman in liner notes to *Miles Davis Quintet, 1965–68.*

18. Interview, *Jazz Profiles*, "Herbie Hancock," National Public Radio, April 2000.

19. "The Magical Journey: An Interview with Wayne Shorter," *Jazz Improv* 2, no. 3 (2000): 72–82.

20. Davis, *Autobiography*, 263.

21. It is noticeable how different the sound is on the LP compared with the CD. Teo Macero encouraged me to listen for this. The sound on

the LP is clearer, crisper, rounder, and with better separation and presence.

22. Frank Tirro uses the word *elastic* to describe some elements of the form of "Circle" in his textbook *Jazz: A History,* 2nd ed. (New York: Norton, 1993), 53.

2. Birth

1. In 1954 Capitol released some of the tracks together. In May of that year they gathered "Venus de Milo," "Rocker," "Jeru," "Godchild," "Rouge," "Deception," "Moon Dreams," and "Israel" for a ten-inch LP in their series *Classics in Jazz.* It was not until 1957 that the remaining instrumental tracks, "Boplicity," "Move," and "Budo," were added, and all eleven (omitting the vocal track) were released on a twelve-inch LP under the title *Birth of the Cool,* apparently coined by Capitol.

2. Pete Welding, liner notes to *Birth of the Cool,* reissue 1989 (Capitol Jazz CDP 7 92862 2).

3. Max Harrison, quoted in Chambers, *Milestones,* 1:106.

4. *New Grove Jazz,* s.v. "Evans, Gil."

5. Chambers, *Milestones,* 1:97.

6. Stephanie Stein Crease, *Gil Evans: Out of the Cool, His Life and Music* (Chicago: A Cappella, 2002), 127–30.

7. Welding, liner notes, *Birth of the Cool.*

8. Gilbert Chase, *America's Music: From the Pilgrims to the Present,* 3rd rev. ed. (Urbana: University of Illinois Press, 1987), 518.

9. *New Grove Jazz,* s.v. "Lewis, John."

10. Chambers, *Milestones,* 1:99.

11. Davis, *Autobiography,* 117.

12. Chambers, *Milestones,* 1:102.

13. Notes by Gerry Mulligan, May 1971, reprinted in liner notes to *Birth of the Cool,* reissue 1989.

14. *New Grove Jazz,* s.v. "Carisi, Johnny."

15. John Szwed, *So What: The Life of Miles Davis* (New York: Simon and Schuster, 2002), 71.

16. Lewis Porter and Michael Ullman, *Jazz: From Its Origins to the Present* (Englewood Cliffs, N.J.: Prentice Hall, 1993), 239–40.

17. *New Grove Jazz*, s.v. "Shearing, George (Albert)."

18. Chambers, *Milestones*, 1:114; André Hodeir, *Jazz: Its Evolution and Essence* (New York: Grove, 1956), 133, 117. See also Don Heckman, "Gil Evans on His Own," in *Jazz Panorama*, ed. Martin T. Williams (New York: Crowell-Collier, 1962), 187–88.

3. Groove

1. *New Grove Jazz*, s. v. "Van Gelder, Rudy."

2. For a detailed discussion of the special features of Van Gelder's sound, see Richard Cook, *Blue Note Records: The Biography* (Boston: Justin, Charles, 2003), 67–69.

3. Davis, *Autobiography*, 129; Chambers, *Milestones*, 1:137, 146.

4. Chambers, *Milestones*, 1:159; Davis, *Autobiography*, 136.

5. Chambers, *Milestones*, 1:175; Davis, *Autobiography*, 127, 169–70.

6. Davis, *Autobiography*, 184, 188.

7. The results were *Blue Haze* (Prestige PRLP 7054—half of the eight tracks on this album had been laid down in 1953), *Walkin'* (Prestige PRLP 7076), *Miles Davis and the Modern Jazz Giants* (Prestige PRLP 7150), and *Bags' Groove* (Prestige PRLP 7109).

8. Davis, *Autobiography*, 187.

9. Chambers, *Milestones*, 1:192, 194; Davis, *Autobiography*, 187.

10. *New Grove Jazz*, s.v. "Monk, Thelonious (Sphere)."

11. *New Grove Jazz*, s.v. "Jackson, Milt(on)."

12. *New Grove Jazz*, s.v. "Heath. (1) Percy Heath (Jr.)."

13. Davis, *Autobiography*, 177.

14. Ibid.

15. The first LP recording in jazz had been with Davis in October 1951 for Prestige (Chambers, *Milestones*, 1:156), but the first significant consequences of the new format for Davis were from April 1954, with "Blue 'n' Boogie" running to a little over eight minutes and "Walkin'" clocking in at thirteen and a half minutes.

16. Postmodern critics have denigrated these qualities in recent commentary. See, e.g., Robert Walser, *Keeping Time: Readings in Jazz History* (New York: Oxford University Press, 1999), 213n2; Lee B. Brown, "Postmodernist Jazz Theory: Afrocentrism, Old and New," *Journal of*

Aesthetics and Art Criticism 57 (1999): 235–46; Samuel A. Floyd Jr., "Ring Shout! Literary Studies, Historical Studies, and Black Music Inquiry," *Black Music Research Journal* 11 (1991): 265–87; Bruce Tucker, editor's introduction, *Black Music Research Journal* (1991), i–vii. Some have gone so far as to close out formal analysis entirely, limiting legitimate forms of enquiry to the sociocultural. See Krin Gabbard, *Jammin' at the Margins: Jazz and the American Cinema* (Chicago: University of Chicago Press, 1996), 1. However ordinary people, musicians, and countless listeners continue to admire unity, coherence, and structure in jazz, ignoring or blissfully unaware of the cramped posturing of revisionist academics. Cannonball Adderley, who would have known, said of Davis: "He thinks a solo can be a composition if it's expressed the right way." See Ira Gitler, "Julian 'Cannonball' Adderley, Part I," *Jazz: A Quarterly of American Music* 3 (1959): 292; quoted in Szwed, *So What*, 163. Brian Harker dismisses the postmodernists far more tactfully than I can manage in his article "Telling a Story: Louis Armstrong and Coherence in Early Jazz," *Current Musicology* 63 (1999): 46–83: " 'Coherence' . . . is just a convenient symbol for a musical reality that . . . Western Europe did not invent and does not own. Whatever we choose to call it, . . . [e]arly jazz musicians hailed [Armstrong] for this achievement [i.e., creating structural coherence], and present-day theorists and historians should do the same—by trying to understand it. The current effort to formulate a culturally based analytical framework for black music can speed this understanding if scholars do not repudiate the *raison d'être* of cultural context: the actual music."

17. Whitney Balliett, quoted in Chambers, *Milestones*, 1:194; Ira Gitler, liner notes to *Bags' Groove* (Prestige PRLP 7109); Ian Carr, *Miles Davis: The Definitive Biography*, rev. ed. (New York: Thunder's Mouth, 1998), 84–85; Max Harrison et al., *Modern Jazz: The Essential Records* (London: Aquarius, 1975), 47; Dick Katz, quoted in Chambers, *Milestones*, 1:193; Porter and Ullman, *Jazz*, 286.

18. Nathaniel Mackey, *Discrepant Engagement: Dissonance, Cross-Culturality, and Experimental Writing* (New York: Cambridge University Press, 1993), 275.

19. This idea is apparently not new, although for some reason it is either underplayed or nonexistent in the standard jazz histories. Frank

Kofsky described "Walkin'" as "the clarion call of the hard bop movement"; Mark Gridley notes that some of the characteristics of hard bop "were also evident in bands which departed more drastically from bop traditions, such as the groups led by Miles Davis between 1955 [sic] and 1961"; Gary Giddins writes that Davis "helped spur and codify the counterrevolution known as 'hard bop' with his 1954 blues 'Walkin'"; and John Szwed claims that "Walkin'" is "widely revered as the recording that opened up a new style of jazz, one that would come to be called hard bop." Frank Kofsky, *Black Nationalism and the Revolution in Music* (New York: Pathfinder, 1970), 35–36; Mark Gridley, *Jazz Styles: History and Analysis*, 7th ed. (Upper Saddle River, N.J.: Prentice Hall, 2000), 208; Gary Giddins, *Visions of Jazz: The First Century* (New York: Oxford University Press, 1998), 341; Szwed, *So What*, 114.

4. Voice

1. Richard Cook writes, "The death of Charlie Parker in 1955 had been the one real watershed of the decade." Cook, *Blue Note Records*, 117.

2. Carr, *Definitive Biography*, 81–82.

3. Chambers, *Milestones*, 1:206.

4. Columbia had already seen how profitable jazz could be with its 1953 signing of Dave Brubeck.

5. Burt Korall, *Drummin' Men, the Heartbeat of Jazz: The Bebop Years* (New York: Oxford University Press, 2002), describes Jones as "the firemaker. He was flexible and confident, often establishing an almost strutting thrust" (230). Korall quotes Jones as saying, "Working with Miles was the greatest thing that ever happened to me" (229).

6. Davis, *Autobiography*, 192. Dan Morgenstern wrote that Chambers was "a marvel who had everything—tone, time, taste, technique—and also was an outstanding soloist." Dan Morgenstern, "Miles Davis," in *Living with Jazz: A Reader* (New York: Pantheon, 2004), 217.

7. Chambers, *Milestones*, 1:214.

8. Ibid., 1:228; Davis, *Autobiography*, 196.

9. *Workin'* (Prestige PRLP 7166), *Steamin'* (Prestige PRLP 7200), *Relaxin'* (Prestige PRLP 7129), and *Cookin'* (Prestige PRLP 7094).

10. Chambers, *Milestones*, 1:240.

11. *Miles Ahead* (Columbia CL 1041).

12. George Avakian, liner notes to the 1993 CD reissue of *Miles Ahead* (Columbia/Legacy CK 53225).

13. Chambers, *Milestones*, 1:260; Art Pepper and Dizzy Gillespie, quoted in Chambers, *Milestones*, 1:261.

14. Whitney Balliett, quoted in Chambers, *Milestones*, 1:260. Ian Carr points out that the idea of a "concerto setting" was "completely fresh," but that the music's "smooth urbanity was not entirely satisfying to Miles," for he needed "the unbridled bite of his open trumpet, and the intense timbre of the Harmon mute." Carr, *Definitive Biography*, 112.

15. Eric Nisenson, *Miles Davis and His Masterpiece: The Making of "Kind of Blue"* (New York: St. Martin's, 2000), 121; Carr, *Definitive Biography*, 117; Davis, *Autobiography*, 193.

16. Ashley Kahn, *"Kind of Blue": The Making of the Miles Davis Masterpiece* (New York: Da Capo, 2000), 167; Davis, *Autobiography*, 223–24.

17. The dates in Chambers, *Milestones*, 1:276 (April 2 and 3) would seem to be in error.

18. *Miles Davis and Milt Jackson Quintet/Sextet* (Prestige PRLP 7034).

19. Davis, *Autobiography*, 221.

20. "Two Bass Hit" was released on *Circle in the Round* (Columbia KC2 36278).

21. Chambers, *Milestones*, 1:224.

22. Davis had used the title "Milestones" for a completely different piece in 1947, recorded for Savoy with Charlie Parker, John Lewis, Nelson Boyd, and Max Roach.

23. Chambers, *Milestones*, 1:279.

24. Davis, *Autobiography*, 220.

25. Carr, *Definitive Biography*, 131.

26. Davis, *Autobiography*, 196–97.

27. Carr, *Definitive Biography*, 99, 114, 116.

5. *Kind of Blue*

1. This quote is printed along with others by George Shearing, Ahmad Jamal, and Cannonball Adderley on the cover of *Everybody Digs*

Bill Evans (Riverside 1129, recorded December 1958), presumably to demonstrate the range and prestige of the diggers.

2. Davis, *Autobiography*, 226.

3. Carr, *Definitive Biography*, 134.

4. Szwed, *So What*, 161.

5. Davis, *Autobiography*, 231.

6. Chambers, *Milestones*, 1:284.

7. Szwed, *So What*, 164; Davis, *Autobiography*, 229. Davis married Frances Taylor in 1960. She had also been a dancer in *West Side Story* during its Broadway run.

8. Carr, *Definitive Biography*, 141.

9. Ralph Ellison and Albert Murray, *Trading Twelves* (New York: Modern Library, 2000), 193, 202.

10. Chambers, *Milestones*, 1:304.

11. Davis, *Autobiography*, 233.

12. The details of the events at both of these sessions have been reconstructed in Kahn's *"Kind of Blue"* and Nisenson's *Miles Davis and His Masterpiece.*

13. Nisenson, *Miles Davis and His Masterpiece*, 147.

14. Kahn, *"Kind of Blue,"* 157.

15. *Metronome*, October 1959, 29; *Down Beat*, October 1, 1959, 28.

16. See David H. Rosenthal, *Hard Bop: Jazz and Black Music, 1955–1965* (New York: Oxford University Press, 1992), 144.

17. Kahn, *"Kind of Blue,"* 194.

18. Szwed, *So What*, 177; Nisenson, *Miles Davis and His Masterpiece*, ix.

6. "There Is No Justice"

1. Carr, *Definitive Biography*, 154–55; Chambers, *Milestones*, 1:313–15; Davis, *Autobiography*, 228–30.

2. Sy Johnson, "An Afternoon at Miles's," *Jazz Magazine*, Fall 1976, 20–27; reprinted in *A Miles Davis Reader*, ed. Bill Kirchner, 198–211 (Washington, D.C.: Smithsonian Institution Press, 1997); LeRoi Jones (Amiri Baraka), "Miles Davis: 'One of the Great Mother Fuckers,'" in Baraka, *The Music: Reflections on Jazz and Blues* (New York: Morrow, 1987), 297–306, reprinted in *A Miles Davis Reader*, ed. Kirchner, 64–73;

Gary Giddins, "Miles to Go, Promises to Keep," *Village Voice*, October 15, 1991, 83, 94–95.

3. Ira Gitler, *Jazz Masters of the Forties* (New York: Macmillan, 1966), 121.

4. Korall, *Drummin' Men*, 131.

5. Davis, *Autobiography*, 222–23.

6. Martin Williams, *The Jazz Tradition* (New York: New American Library, 1970), 160.

7. Davis, *Autobiography*, 232. Davis also said, "Flamenco is the Spanish counterpart of our blues." *Down Beat*, October 27, 1960.

8. Chambers, *Milestones*, 2:12.

9. Macero earned both a bachelor's and a master's degree from the Juilliard School of Music and was one of the founding members of Charles Mingus's Jazz Composers Workshop. He performed and recorded with Mingus on both tenor and baritone sax, and as a composer he was involved in the Third Stream movement with Gunther Schuller. He brought Mingus into the Columbia fold and worked on recordings of Mingus, Brubeck, Monk, and many others. Carr, *Definitive Biography*, 157, 159; *New Grove Jazz*, s.v. "Macero, Teo"; interview conducted with Teo Macero, March 31, 2000.

10. I could not disagree more with Carr's overview of this period. He would see the small-group recordings as "preparations" for the orchestral recordings of 1958–60. Similarly (and, in my view, erroneously), he believes that the small-group recordings of 1964–67 are "preparation" for the work of the late 1960s: *Miles in the Sky, Bitches Brew*, etc. See Carr, *Definitive Biography*, 161–62.

11. Davis, *Autobiography*, 236.

7. Not Happening

1. Chambers, *Milestones*, 2:5, 6, 16–17. The split had even been announced before the tour in the *Philadelphia Tribune* and *Down Beat*. See Lewis Porter, *John Coltrane: His Life and Music* (Ann Arbor: University of Michigan Press, 1998), 142.

2. At the end of 1965, the readers' poll in *Down Beat* voted John Coltrane first in the Hall of Fame, Jazzman of the Year, leader of the

record of the year for *A Love Supreme,* and first for tenor saxophone. Carr, *Definitive Biography,* 203.

3. "Miles . . . almost broke down and wept during their last gig together, in Philadelphia. So strongly did he feel that he even went to the microphone and made a brief announcement about the saxophonist's imminent departure from the group. And as Jimmy Cobb commented: 'He never talks with nobody about nothing, so you know, he really must have felt something for Coltrane.' " Carr, *Definitive Biography,* 168.

4. Ralph Gleason, *Celebrating the Duke* (New York: Dell, 1975), 139.

5. Chambers, *Milestones,* 2:3–75.

6. Joe Goldberg, *Jazz Masters of the Fifties* (New York: Macmillan, 1965), 231.

7. A. B. Spellman, *Four Lives in the Bebop Business* (New York: Schocken, 1966), 14.

8. *Down Beat,* June 13, 1964.

9. Harvey Pekar wrote that Davis's "bent for experimentation seems to have temporarily left him." See Pekar, "1964–69 Recordings." Chambers writes that "for the first and only time in his career Davis was willing to stand aside and allow the innovations to proceed without him." Chambers, *Milestones,* 2:24.

10. Davis, *Autobiography,* 246–47.

11. Leonard Feather, "Miles and the Fifties," *Down Beat,* July 2, 1964, 44–48, 98.

12. Davis, *Autobiography,* 240–41.

13. "Playboy Interview: Miles Davis," *Playboy,* September 1962. In part, this may also have been because Davis thought of the magazine as racially biased. " 'All they have . . . are blond women with big tits and flat asses or no asses. . . . Black guys like big asses, you know, and we like to kiss on the mouth and white women don't have no mouths to kiss on.' " Davis, *Autobiography,* 250.

14. Roger Cotterrell, "Interlude: Miles Davis with Hank Mobley," *Jazz Monthly,* October 1967, 3–4.

15. *Someday* (Columbia CL 1656), *Quiet Nights* (CL 2106), and *Seven Steps* (CL 2051).

16. Blackhawk (Columbia C2L20), Carnegie (Columbia CS 8612), and Philharmonic (Columbia CL 2453, CL 2306). Music from a two-week

engagement at the Plugged Nickel in Chicago at the end of 1965 was only released much later: two LPs in Japan in 1976 (CBS-Sony 25 AP 1 and 25 AP 291), released in the United States by Columbia as a double album in 1982 (Columbia C2 38266) and an eight-CD set of two complete nights put out by Sony in 1995: *Miles Davis: The Complete Live at the Plugged Nickel 1965* (Columbia/Legacy CXK-66595).

17. Released by CBS as *Miles à Antibes* (CBS [France] 62390) and by Columbia as *Miles Davis in Europe* (Columbia CS 8993); *Miles in Tokyo: Miles Davis Live in Concert* (CBS-Sony SOPL 162); and *Miles in Berlin* (CBS [Germany] S 62976/62104). The Tokyo and Berlin records were reissued in 1983 as a double album, *Miles Davis: Heard 'Round the World* (Columbia C2 38506).

A study of these recordings shows Davis starting to play in a more experimental manner; Coleman (at Antibes) uninspiring (most notably on "Milestones," where he seems mostly to be working on his scales); Tony Williams coming strongly into his own, especially behind the solos in Tokyo and Berlin; Sam Rivers and Davis playing beautifully in Tokyo; and (only two months later) one of the earliest appearances of the quintet with Wayne Shorter (Berlin), whose completely original conception and mastery of Davis "classics" such as "Walkin' " and "Milestones" give the group a significantly new sound. The music on these albums is finally available on CD: *Seven Steps: The Complete Columbia Recordings of Miles Davis, 1963–1964* (Columbia/Legacy C7K90840).

18. Even Howard Brofsky, in "Miles Davis and *My Funny Valentine:* The Evolution of a Solo," *Black Music Research Journal* 3 (1983): 23–45, does not seem aware of this performance.

19. Cotterrell, "Interlude: Miles Davis with Hank Mobley."

20. On the album *My Favorite Things* (Atlantic 1361).

21. As Max Harrison pointed out, "Surely *Quiet Nights* should be regarded as an emblematic failure, signaling the partnership's [i.e., that between Davis and Gil Evans] effective end." See Max Harrison, "Sheer Alchemy, for a While: Miles Davis and Gil Evans," in *A Jazz Retrospect* (Boston: Crescendo, 1976); revised and reprinted in *A Miles Davis Reader,* ed. Bill Kirchner (Washington, D.C.: Smithsonian Institution Press, 1997), 75–103.

22. See Chambers, *Milestones,* 2:48.

23. The company also had to resort to compilations of earlier material. In 1963 they released *Basic Miles: The Classic Performances of Miles Davis* (Columbia PC 32025) with material from 1955, 1956, 1957, 1958, and 1962 and *Miles Davis: Facets* (CBS [France] 62637) with material from 1956 and 1958.

24. Davis, *Autobiography,* 63.

25. Interview, *Jazz Profiles,* "Wayne Shorter," National Public Radio, February 2000.

26. Tapes were made of concerts in Los Angeles, Berlin, Paris, Stockholm, Copenhagen, Sindelfingen (Germany), Milan, and San Francisco. See Jan Lohmann, *The Sound of Miles Davis: The Discography: A Listing of Records and Tapes, 1945–1991* (Copenhagen: JazzMedia, n.d.), 88–91. The Berlin performances were released on the *Miles in Berlin* album, the easiest way to hear the group together for the first time.

27. Scott Yanow, "Miles Davis: The Later Years," *Record Review,* April 1978, 58; Chambers, *Milestones,* 2:88.

28. Ron Carter is responsible for three of the pieces, Shorter for two, and Davis and Hancock for one each.

29. Yanow ("The Later Years," 59) dubbed *Miles Smiles* "the essential quintet album from this period." His review in 1992 called *Miles Smiles* "a gem" and "arguably [the quintet's] most rewarding recording." See *Cadence* 18 (June 1992): 28. Michael Ullman, however, gave the record faint praise, labeling it with the black-hole characterization "transitional." See Michael Ullman, "Miles Davis in Retrospect," *New Boston Review,* May/June 1981: 18–20; reprinted in *A Miles Davis Reader,* ed. Bill Kirchner (Washington, D.C.: Smithsonian Institution Press, 1997), 8–14. Amiri Baraka was no more insightful, calling Davis's music of the mid-1960s "the hip restatement of [the] classic period [of the first quintet and the sextet]," which is more or less exactly what it was not. See Baraka, "One of the Great."

30. Chambers, *Milestones,* 2:108; Carr, *Definitive Biography,* 206–207.

31. Todd Coolman, "The Miles Davis Quintet of the Mid-1960s: Synthesis of Improvisational and Compositional Elements" (Ph.D. diss., New York University, 1997), 26.

8. The Second Quintet

1. "Blue X-mas (To Whom It May Concern)," "Nothing Like You," and "Devil May Care" with Frank Rehak (trombone), Bob Dorough (piano, vocal), Paul Chambers (bass), Jimmy Cobb (drums), and William Correa (Willie Bobo) (congas), recorded in New York on August 21 and 23, 1962.

2. Shorter recalled the contrast between Blakey's and Davis's groups: "It wasn't the bish-bash, sock-'em-dead routine we had with Blakey, with every solo a climax. With Miles, I felt like a cello, I felt viola, I felt liquid, dot-dash . . . and colors started really coming." *Down Beat*, July 14, 1977.

3. Tony Williams plays on *My Point of View,* and both Ron Carter and Williams play on *Empyrean Isles* and *Maiden Voyage.*

4. Blue Note BLP 4180 and BLP 4216. Williams used Sam Rivers as saxophonist as well as Herbie Hancock on piano on both these albums. Wayne Shorter also plays on *Spring.*

5. Davis, *Autobiography,* 252, 254.

6. Carr, *Definitive Biography,* 12–16.

7. Bennie Maupin has spoken of Hancock's interest in classical music in the 1960s: "He was very into . . . Stravinsky and Mahler, as well as Ravel and Debussy, and I could hear those influences in his playing." Interview, *Jazz Profiles,* "Herbie Hancock," National Public Radio, April 2000.

8. George Goodman Jr., "Miles Davis: 'I Just Pick Up My Horn and Play,'" *New York Times,* June 28, 1981. Christopher Smith has written well of Davis creating a kind of "ritual space" for his performances; see his "A Sense of the Possible: Miles Davis and the Semiotics of Improvised Performance," *Drama Review* 39 (1995): 41–55.

9. Davis, *Autobiography,* 220.

10. Carr, *Definitive Biography,* 190.

11. See Bob Belden, liner notes to *Miles Davis Quintet, 1965–68.*

12. Quoted in Ralph Gleason, liner notes to *Friday Night at the Blackhawk* and *Saturday Night at the Blackhawk,* Columbia 44257 and 44425, reprinted as "At the Blackhawk" in *The Miles Davis Companion,* ed. Gary Carner (New York: Schirmer, 1996), 82–85.

9. The Album *Miles Smiles*, Side 1

1. The six records contain sixteen compositions by Shorter, thirteen by Davis, four by Hancock, three by Carter, and three by Williams.

2. Analysis of "Orbits" has caused difficulties. Douglas Clark describes it as "dodecaphonic (but not serial)," and Chambers writes that it "seems to keep its structural secrets hidden after repeated listening." Douglas Clark, "Miles into Jazz-Rock Territory," *Jazz Journal* 30 (June 1977): 13; Chambers, *Milestones*, 99.

3. I am grateful to Zbigniew Granat for this observation.

4. Following the lead of Elvin Jones, Williams used a small wooden-shelled drum set with a smaller than usual bass drum of 14"×18" and K. Zildjian cymbals made in Turkey. See Joe Hunt, *52nd Street Beat: In-depth Profiles of Modern Jazz Drummers, 1945–1965* (New Albany, Ind.: Aebersold, n.d.), 24. The smaller bass drum and the rich cymbal timbre made for a more colorful midrange set of instruments, out of the way of the bass and into the "participatory" area of the texture.

5. Anthony Tuttle, liner notes to the LP *Miles Smiles* (Columbia CS 9401); Chambers, *Milestones*, 99.

6. Herbie Hancock has described how "Circle" was partially derived from "Drad-Dog." See the liner notes to *Miles Davis Quintet, 1965–68*.

7. See Tirro, *Jazz: A History*, 54. Tirro analyzes "Circle" in his book, and I am indebted to his work, although our perceptions differ in certain respects. Other views on the piece are more ambivalent. Bill Cole regarded it as "a beautiful composition" but "not very innovative." See his *Miles Davis: A Musical Biography* (New York: William Morrow, 1985), 159–60.

8. Bob Belden, liner notes to *Miles Davis Quintet, 1965–68*.

9. The increasing fashion, initiated some twenty years ago by Gunther Schuller and continued most notably by Billy Taylor and others (see, e.g., Grover Sales, *Jazz: America's Classical Music* [Englewood Cliffs, N.J.: Prentice Hall, 1984] and Billy Taylor, "Jazz: America's Classical Music," *Black Perspectives in Music* 14 [1986]: 21–25) for describing jazz as "America's classical music" is deeply misguided. It is but a continuation of the

inferiority complex suffered by jazz vis-à-vis the concert hall since its inception. Walser has a similar take on this—see *Keeping Time*, 347–50—and Scott DeVeaux has sketched the limitations of the classicizing approach in his article "Constructing the Jazz Tradition: Jazz Historiography," *Black American Literature Forum* 25 (1991): 525–60. See also Alex Ross, "Classical View: Talking Some Good, Hard Truths about Music," *New York Times,* November 12, 1995, sec. 2, 35; Clive Davis, "Has Jazz Gone Classical?" *Wilson Quarterly* 21 (1997): 56–63; and Jon Pareles, "Don't Call Jazz America's Classical Music," *New York Times,* February 28, 1999, sec. 2, 38.

10. Interview, *Jazz Profiles,* "Herbie Hancock," National Public Radio, April 2000.

11. Personal communication.

12. We will see below how an insensitive but "conscientious" producer might have made it considerably shorter.

13. A jazz composition that is, in the conventional parlance, "modal" should be distinguished from one that is composed in a mode. The former may use modal chords, but it is "modal" because of its areas of several measures of unchanging harmony and its lack of conventional chord progressions. A piece composed in a mode may also use modal chords (usually based on fourths), but its progressions are more traditional.

14. Scott DeVeaux kindly pointed out the source of this quotation.

15. I am grateful to Lisa Scoggin for helping to illuminate the rhythmic details of this performance. In the literature there are only two vague references to this shift. In his 1976 *Coda* article "Miles Davis: 1964–69 Recordings," Harvey Pekar writes: " 'Footprints,' by Shorter, is a 6/4 blues. However, there is some use of 4/4 as well as 6/4 meter during the improvised section of 'Footprints.' " And in *Miles Davis: Sein Leben, Seine Musik, Seine Schallplatten,* 2nd ed. (Schaftlach: Oreos, 1988), Peter Weismüller notes, "During certain passages of improvisation, the rhythm section changes into a 4/4 beat and thereby attains a liveliness that despite the impassioned delivery of the horn solos almost pushes them out of the limelight" ["Während einiger Improvisationspassagen wechselt die Rhythmusgruppe in einen 4/4-Takt und erreicht damit eine Lebendigkeit, die die Bläsersoli trotz ihres passionierten Vortrages fast aus dem Rampenlicht drängt"] (168). Pekar also writes that the

playing of the rhythm section on this track is "one of the very greatest in jazz history."

16. *Miles Smiles* (reissue, Columbia/Legacy CK 48849). The *Miles Smiles* numbers on the boxed set follow the LP exactly in terms of the length of each track.

17. Interview of March 31, 2000.

18. *Adam's Apple*, Blue Note BLP 4232, reissued as CDP 7 46403-2. This album was recorded on February 3 and 24, 1966.

19. These references may also be heard as atavisms of Shorter's earlier solo.

10. The Album *Miles Smiles*, Side 2

1. See Chambers, *Milestones*, 2:99. He is wrong, however, in stating that the whole of the composed portion of "Dolores" amounts to no more than eight measures.

2. It is a measure of the abstract nature of most of the playing on this album how rare such melodic reference is. The only other examples I can hear are the Ellington reference in "Footprints" and the quotation in Hancock's solo on "Ginger Bread Boy." I wish I could identify the source of the quotation here. . . .

3. "The Magical Journey: An Interview with Wayne Shorter," in *Jazz Improv* 2, no. 3 (2000): 75.

4. *The Best of Eddie Harris* (Vee-Jay VJ 1448, also available on Atlantic Jazz 1545-2). Harris first became famous from his recording of the theme from the film *Exodus* in 1961 (Vee-Jay VJ 3036).

5. Hancock said that Davis was "a master at being able to conceptualize a composition—someone else's composition—understand the heart of it and reshape it to get the most value out of it." Carr, *Definitive Biography*, 207.

6. Richard Cook beautifully describes Hancock's contribution as "doomy, tolling chords." Cook, *It's About That Time*, 177.

7. "For many people, 'Footprints' and 'Freedom Jazz Dance' expressed the musical essence of a period; they created reference points, standards against which other performances were judged." Carr, *Definitive Biography*, 206.

8. Gridley, in *Jazz Styles,* describes the playing of Williams as "overflow[ing] with imagination" and points out that his high-hat timekeeping on this track was "later adopted by hundreds of jazz-rock drummers" (244).

9. Although the solo covers two octaves, it lies mostly in the middle tenth of that range.

10. Peter Weismüller draws attention to this technique: "In the improvisations the soloists tend strongly towards the recollection of thematic fragments. Freed from the constraint of harmonic progression, this conceptual development—melodic improvisation—harks back paradoxically to the roots of jazz." ["In den Improvisationen tendieren die Solisten verstärkt zur Rückbesinnung auf thematische Fragmente. Befreit vom Zwang der harmonischen Sequenz verweist dieser konzeptionelle Fortschritt—die melodische Improvisation—paradoxerweise auf die Wurzeln des Jazz zurück."] *Miles Davis: Sein Leben,* 168.

11. *Young Man with a Horn* (Blue Note BN 5022).

12. "Ginger Bread Boy" appeared on the album and the 1992 reissue, but it was rendered "Gingerbread Boy" in the box set and on some lead sheets.

13. *On the Trail* (Riverside RLP-9486, reissued on OJCCD-1854-2).

14. See Belden's liner notes to *Miles Davis Quintet, 1965–68.*

15. Hancock quoted in Coolman, "Miles Davis Quintet," 27.

16. I would be delighted to hear from any reader who can identify this quote and the one in Example 18.

17. Producer Michael Cuscuna has said: "I think what that group did was it truly raised the bar for jazz. I don't think that ever before had musicianship, by every member of the band, been at such a high level." Interview, *Jazz Profiles,* "Herbie Hancock," National Public Radio, April 2000.

18. See Porter, *John Coltrane,* 201. Eric Nisenson (*'Round About Midnight,* 192) describes Coltrane's quartet as "the dominant jazz unit of the sixties."

19. I have pointed out above (see chapter 9, note 4) how Tony Williams, perhaps the *primus inter pares* of Davis's quintet, used the same drum set as Elvin Jones. Clearly, coming up in the early 1960s, Williams must have been strongly influenced by Elvin Jones, who had

already made his mark as an independent and original drummer in the late 1950s, playing with Sonny Rollins, J. J. Johnson, Pepper Adams, and Tommy Flanagan.

20. Elvin Jones, liner notes to *Coltrane: The Classic Quartet—Complete Impulse! Studio Recordings*. Impulse! IMPD 8-280.

21. Other borrowings are suggested by Franz Kerschbaumer in his article "Zum Personalstil von Miles Davis," *Jazzforschung* 3/4 (1971/72): 225–32; e.g., "This example ['Bye, Bye, Blackbird'] shows that Davis had already absorbed modal influences that probably came primarily from Coltrane." ["Dieses Beispiel zeigt, daß Davis bereits modale Einflüsse aufgenommen hat, die hier wohl in erster Linie von Coltrane ausgegangen sind."] (232).

22. Original albums: AS-21, AS-32, AS-42, AS-66, AS-77, and AS-85. All the sessions have been issued on *Coltrane: The Classic Quartet—Complete Impulse! Studio Recordings*. Impulse! IMPD 8-280. Nisenson describes Davis's quintet as being "overshadowed" by Coltrane's quartet. *'Round About Midnight*, 192.

23. Don Heckman once compared Davis's style to that of Ernest Hemingway. "Like Hemingway, Davis is wry, epigrammatic, witty; he minces neither words nor phrases [and] seldom plays notes that are unnecessary." See Don Heckman, "Miles Davis Times Three: The Evolution of a Jazz Artist," *Down Beat*, August 30, 1962, 16–19; reprinted in *A Miles Davis Reader*, ed. Bill Kirchner (Washington D.C.: Smithsonian, 1997), 110–22.

24. Shorter describes his reaction upon hearing Davis for the first time: "I wondered what it was when they said this trumpet player was making a whole lot of mistakes. His name was Miles Davis. [*laughs*] . . . 'He doesn't *sound* like a trumpet player at all!' Miles always said that: 'You know, I'm *not* a trumpet player. I don't play the trumpet.' . . . He said that the trumpet was just a tool . . . a magic wand!" "The Magical Journey," 72–74.

25. See Eddie Meadows, "The Miles Davis–Wayne Shorter Connection: Continuity and Change," *Jazzforschung* 20 (1988): 58.

26. Troupe, *Miles and Me*, 70.

Conclusion

1. This pattern of taking energy from younger players was often re-peated as Davis got older.

2. The standard histories, relating the transition from the expanded quintet to the bigger studio groups of *In a Silent Way* and *Bitches Brew,* tend to omit mention of one more quintet with which Davis toured in 1969. Peter Keepnews has called this group the "Last Quintet" or the "Lost Quintet." It was made up of Davis, Shorter, Chick Corea, Dave Holland, and Jack DeJohnette, and it was on the road a lot in 1969, but (apart from some bootleg recordings and some private tapes) it was never recorded. See Peter Keepnews, "The Lost Quintet," in *Village Voice Jazz Supplement: Miles Davis at 60,* August 1986, 22–23.

Bibliography

Books and Articles

Avakian, George. Liner notes to the 1993 CD reissue of *Miles Ahead*. Columbia/Legacy CK 53225.

Belden, Bob. Liner notes to *Miles Davis Quintet, 1965–68*. Columbia 4-67398.

Brofsky, Howard. "Miles Davis and *My Funny Valentine:* The Evolution of a Solo." *Black Music Research Journal* 3 (1983): 23–45.

Brown, Lee B. "Postmodernist Jazz Theory: Afrocentrism, Old and New." *Journal of Aesthetics and Art Criticism* 57 (1999): 235–46.

Carr, Ian. *Miles Davis: The Definitive Biography.* Rev. ed. New York: Thunder's Mouth Press, 1998.

Chambers, Jack. *Milestones: The Music and Times of Miles Davis.* 2 vols. Toronto: University of Toronto Press, 1989; reprint, New York: Da Capo, 1998.

Chase, Gilbert. *America's Music: From the Pilgrims to the Present.* 3rd rev. ed. Urbana: University of Illinois, 1987.

Clark, Douglas. "Miles into Jazz-Rock Territory." *Jazz Journal* 30 (1977): 12–14.

Cole, Bill. *Miles Davis: A Musical Biography.* New York: William Morrow, 1985.

Cook, Richard. *Blue Note Records: The Biography.* Boston: Justin, Charles, 2003.

———. *It's About That Time: Miles Davis On and Off Record.* New York: Oxford University Press, 2007.

Coolman, Todd. Liner notes to *Miles Davis Quintet, 1965–68*. Columbia 4-67398.

———. "The Miles Davis Quintet of the Mid-1960s: Synthesis of Improvisational and Compositional Elements." Ph.D. diss., New York University, 1997.

Cotterrell, Roger. "Interlude: Miles Davis with Hank Mobley." *Jazz Monthly*, October 1967, 3–4.

Crease, Stephanie Stein. *Gil Evans: Out of the Cool, His Life and Music.* Chicago: A Cappella, 2002.

Davis, Clive. "Has Jazz Gone Classical?" *Wilson Quarterly* 21 (1997): 56–63.

Davis, Miles, with Quincy Troupe. *Miles: The Autobiography.* New York: Simon and Schuster, 1989.

DeVeaux, Scott. "Constructing the Jazz Tradition: Jazz Historiography." *Black American Literature Forum* 25 (1991): 525–60.

Ellison, Ralph, and Albert Murray. *Trading Twelves.* New York: Modern Library, 2000.

Feather, Leonard. "Miles and the Fifties." *Down Beat,* July 2, 1964, 44–48, 98.

Floyd, Samuel A., Jr. "Ring Shout! Literary Studies, Historical Studies, and Black Music Inquiry." *Black Music Research Journal* 11 (1991): 265–87.

Gabbard, Krin. *Jammin' at the Margins: Jazz and the American Cinema.* Chicago: Chicago University Press, 1996.

Gerard, Charley. *Jazz in Black and White: Race, Culture, and Identity in the Jazz Community.* Westport, Conn.: Praeger, 1998.

Giddins, Gary. "Miles to Go, Promises to Keep." *Village Voice,* October 15, 1991, 83, 94–95.

———. *Visions of Jazz: The First Century.* New York: Oxford University Press, 1998.

Gitler, Ira. *Jazz Masters of the Forties.* New York: Macmillan, 1966.

———. "Julian 'Cannonball' Adderley, Part I." *Jazz: A Quarterly of American Music* 3 (1959): 201–203, 291–92.

———. Liner notes to *Bags' Groove.* Prestige LP 7109.

Gleason, Ralph. *Celebrating the Duke.* New York: Dell, 1975.

———. Liner notes to *Friday Night at the Blackhawk* and *Saturday Night at the Blackhawk.* Columbia 44257 and 44425. Reprinted as "At the Blackhawk," in *The Miles Davis Companion: Four Decades of Commentary,* ed. Gary Carner, 82–85. New York: Schirmer, 1996.

Gioia, Ted. *The History of Jazz.* New York: Oxford University Press, 1997.

Goldberg, Joe. *Jazz Masters of the Fifties.* New York: Macmillan, 1965.

Goodman, George, Jr. "Miles Davis: 'I Just Pick Up My Horn and Play.'" *New York Times,* June 28, 1981.

Gray, Herman. "Jazz Tradition, Institutional Formation, and Cultural Practice: The Canon and the Street as Frameworks for Oppositional Black Cultural Politics." In *From Sociology to Cultural Studies: New Perspectives,* ed. Elizabeth Long, 351–73. Malden, Mass.: Blackwell, 1997.

Gridley, Mark. *Jazz Styles: History and Analysis.* 7th ed. Upper Saddle River, N.J.: Prentice Hall, 2000.

Harker, Brian. "Telling a Story: Louis Armstrong and Coherence in Early Jazz." *Current Musicology* 63 (1999): 46–83.

Harrison, Max. "Sheer Alchemy, for a While: Miles Davis and Gil Evans." In *A Jazz Retrospect.* Boston: Crescendo, 1976. Revision in *A Miles Davis Reader,* ed. Bill Kirchner, 75–103. Washington, D.C.: Smithsonian Institution Press, 1997.

Harrison, Max, et al. *Modern Jazz: The Essential Records.* London: Aquarius, 1975.

Hasse, John Edward. *Beyond Category: The Life and Genius of Duke Ellington.* New York: Da Capo, 1995.

Heckman, Don. "Gil Evans on His Own." In *Jazz Panorama,* ed. Martin T. Williams. New York: Crowell-Collier, 1962.

———. "Miles Davis Times Three: The Evolution of a Jazz Artist." *Down Beat,* August 30, 1962, 16–19. Reprint in *A Miles Davis Reader,* ed. Bill Kirchner, 110–22. Washington, D.C.: Smithsonian, 1997.

Hodeir, André. *Jazz: Its Evolution and Essence.* New York: Grove, 1956.

Hunt, Joe. *52nd Street Beat: In-depth Profiles of Modern Jazz Drummers, 1945–1965.* New Albany, Ind.: Aebersold, n.d.

Johnson, Sy. "An Afternoon at Miles's." *Jazz Magazine,* Fall 1976, 20–27. Reprint in *A Miles Davis Reader,* ed. Bill Kirchner, 198–211. Washington, D.C.: Smithsonian Institution Press, 1997.

Jones, Elvin. Epigraph to liner notes to *Coltrane: The Classic Quartet— Complete Impulse! Studio Recordings.* Impulse! IMPD 8-280.

Jones, LeRoi (Amiri Baraka). "Miles Davis: 'One of the Great Mother Fuckers.'" In *The Music: Reflections on Jazz and Blues,* 297–306. New York: Morrow, 1987. Reprinted in *A Miles Davis Reader,* ed. Bill Kirchner, 63–73. Washington, D.C.: Smithsonian Institution Press, 1997.

Kahn, Ashley. *"Kind of Blue": The Making of the Miles Davis Masterpiece.* New York: Da Capo, 2000.

Keepnews, Peter. "The Lost Quintet." *Village Voice Jazz Supplement: Miles Davis at 60,* August 1986, 22–23.

Kerschbaumer, Franz. "Zum Personalstil von Miles Davis." *Jazzforschung* 3/4 (1971/72): 225–32.

Kirchner, Bill, ed. *A Miles Davis Reader.* Washington, D.C.: Smithsonian Institution Press, 1997.

Kofsky, Frank. *Black Nationalism and the Revolution in Music.* New York: Pathfinder, 1970.

Korall, Burt. *Drummin' Men, the Heartbeat of Jazz: The Bebop Years.* New York: Oxford University Press, 2002.

Litweiler, John. *The Freedom Principle: Jazz after 1958.* New York: William Morrow, 1984.

Lohmann, Jan. *The Sound of Miles Davis: The Discography: A Listing of Records and Tapes, 1945–1991.* Copenhagen: JazzMedia, n.d.

Mackey, Nathaniel. *Discrepant Engagement: Dissonance, Cross-Culturality, and Experimental Writing.* New York: Cambridge University Press, 1993.

Meadows, Eddie. "The Miles Davis–Wayne Shorter Connection: Continuity and Change." *Jazzforschung* 20 (1988): 58.

Mialy, Louis-Victor. "Ron Carter: Un géant des profondeurs." *Jazz Hot,* May 1983, 400.

Morgenstern, Dan. "Miles Davis." In *Living with Jazz: A Reader,* 206–21. New York: Pantheon, 2004.

Mulligan, Gerry. Notes of May 1971. Reprint. Liner notes to *Birth of the Cool.* Reissue 1989. Capitol Jazz CDP 7 92862 2.

The New Grove Dictionary of Jazz. 2nd ed. Edited by Barry Kernfeld. New York: St. Martin's, 2002.

Nisenson, Eric. *Miles Davis and His Masterpiece: The Making of "Kind of Blue."* New York: St. Martin's, 2000.

———. *'Round About Midnight: A Portrait of Miles Davis.* New York: Dial, 1982.

Pareles, Jon. "Don't Call Jazz America's Classical Music." *New York Times,* February 28, 1999, sec. 2, 38.

Pekar, Harvey. "Miles Davis: 1964–69 Recordings." *Coda,* May 1976, 8–14. Reprint in *A Miles Davis Reader,* ed. Bill Kirchner, 164–83. Washington, D.C.: Smithsonian Institution Press, 1997.

Porter, Lewis. *John Coltrane: His Life and Music.* Ann Arbor: University of Michigan Press, 1998.

Porter, Lewis, and Michael Ullman. *Jazz: From Its Origins to the Present.* Englewood Cliffs, N.J.: Prentice Hall, 1993.

Rosenthal, David H. *Hard Bop: Jazz and Black Music, 1955–1965.* New York: Oxford University Press, 1992.

Ross, Alex. "Classical View: Talking Some Good, Hard Truths about Music." *New York Times,* November 12, 1995, sec. 2, 35.

Roszczuk, Antoni. "Teo Macero: 'A Producer Must Encourage the Artist to Do New Things.'" *Jazz Forum: The Magazine of the International Jazz Federation* 50 (1977): 39.

Rygalyk, Rainer (R.E.). "Miles Never Smiles." *JazzLive,* July/August 1984, 4–6.

Sales, Grover. *Jazz: America's Classical Music.* Englewood Cliffs, N.J.: Prentice Hall, 1984.

Shaw, Arnold. *52nd St.: The Street of Jazz.* New York: Da Capo, 1977. Originally published as *The Street That Never Slept.* New York: Coward, McCann, and Geoghegan, 1971.

Smith, Christopher. "A Sense of the Possible: Miles Davis and the Semiotics of Improvised Performance." *Drama Review* 39 (1995): 41–55.

Spellman, A. B. *Four Lives in the Bebop Business.* New York: Schocken, 1966.

Szwed, John. *So What: The Life of Miles Davis.* New York: Simon and Schuster, 2002.

Taylor, Billy. "Jazz: America's Classical Music." *Black Perspectives in Music* 14 (1986): 21–25.

Tirro, Frank. *Jazz: A History.* 2nd ed. New York: Norton, 1993.

Troupe, Quincy. *Miles and Me.* Berkeley: University of California Press, 2000.

Tucker, Bruce. Editor's introduction. *Black Music Research Journal* 11 (1991): i–vii.

Tuttle, Anthony. Liner notes to *Miles Smiles.* Columbia CL 2601/CS 9401.

Ullman, Michael. "Miles Davis in Retrospect." *New Boston Review,* May/June 1981, 18–20. Reprint in *A Miles Davis Reader,* ed. Bill Kirchner, 8–14. Washington, D.C.: Smithsonian Institution Press, 1997.

Walser, Robert. *Keeping Time: Readings in Jazz History.* New York: Oxford University Press, 1999.

Weismüller, Peter. *Miles Davis: Sein Leben, Seine Musik, Seine Schallplatten.* 2nd ed. Schaftlach: Oreos, 1988.

Welding, Pete. Liner notes to *Birth of the Cool.* Reissue 1989. Capitol Jazz CDP 7 92862 2.

Williams, Martin. *The Jazz Tradition.* New York: New American Library, 1970.

Yanow, Scott. "Miles Davis: The Later Years." *Record Review,* April 1978, 58–59.

———. Review of *Miles Smiles. Cadence* 18 (1992): 28.

Interviews

Carter, Ron. *Jazz Profiles,* "Herbie Hancock," National Public Radio, April 2000.

Cuscuna, Michael. *Jazz Profiles,* "Herbie Hancock," National Public Radio, April 2000.

Davis, Miles. *Down Beat,* June 13, 1964.

———. *Playboy,* September 1962.

Macero, Teo. With author, March 31, 2000.

Maupin, Bennie. *Jazz Profiles,* "Herbie Hancock," National Public Radio, April 2000.

Metheny, Pat. *Jazz Profiles,* "Herbie Hancock," National Public Radio, April 2000.

Shorter, Wayne. *Jazz Profiles,* "Wayne Shorter," National Public Radio, February 2000.

———. "The Magical Journey: An Interview with Wayne Shorter." In *Jazz Improv* 2, no. 3 (2000): 72–82.

Select Discography

Miles Davis

Basic Miles: The Classic Performances of Miles Davis. Columbia PC 32025.

Circle in the Round. Columbia KC2 36278.

Directions. Columbia KC2 36474.

E.S.P. Columbia CS 9150.

Filles de Kilimanjaro. Columbia CS 34396.

Friday Night at the Blackhawk. Columbia 44257.

Miles à Antibes. CBS (France) 62390. (= *Miles Davis in Europe.* Columbia CS 8993.)

Miles Ahead. Columbia CL 1041.

Miles Davis: Facets. CBS (France) 62637.

Miles Davis: Heard 'Round the World. Columbia C2 38506.

Miles Davis: The Complete Live at the Plugged Nickel, 1965. Columbia/ Legacy 66595.

Miles Davis Quintet, 1965–68. Columbia 4-67398.

Miles in Berlin. CBS (Germany) S 62976/62104.

Miles Davis in Europe. Columbia CS 8993. (= *Miles à Antibes.* CBS [France] 62390.)

Miles in the Sky. Columbia CS 9628.

Miles in Tokyo: Miles Davis Live in Concert. CBS-Sony SOPL 162.

Miles Smiles. Columbia CL 2601.

Miles Smiles. Reissue, Columbia CS 9401.

Miles Smiles. Reissue, Columbia/Legacy CK 48849.

Nefertiti. Columbia CS 9594.

Quiet Nights. Columbia CL 2106.

Saturday Night at the Blackhawk. Columbia 44425.

Seven Steps: The Complete Columbia Recordings of Miles Davis, 1963–1964. Columbia/Legacy C7K90840.

Seven Steps to Heaven. Columbia CL 2051.

Someday My Prince Will Come. Columbia CL 1656.

Sorcerer. Columbia CS 9532.

Water Babies. Columbia C 34396.

Young Man with a Horn. Blue Note BN 5022.

John Coltrane

Ballads. Impulse! A-32.

Coltrane. Impulse! A-21.

Crescent. Impulse! A-66.

Impressions. Impulse! A-42.

The John Coltrane Quartet Plays. Impulse! A-85.

A Love Supreme. Impulse! A-77.

[All reissued in *Coltrane—The Classic Quartet: The Complete Impulse! Studio Recordings*. Impulse! IMPD 8-280.]

Herbie Hancock

Empyrean Isles. Blue Note BLP 4175. CDP 7 84175-2.

Maiden Voyage. Blue Note BLP 4195. CDP 7 46339-2.

My Point of View. Blue Note BLP 4126.

Takin' Off. Blue Note BLP 4109. CDP 7243 8 37643-2.

Eddie Harris

The Best of Eddie Harris. Vee-Jay VJ 1448. Reissue, Atlantic Jazz 1545-2.

Exodus to Jazz. Vee-Jay VJ 3036. Reissue, NVJ2-904.

Jimmy Heath

On the Trail. Riverside RLP-9486. Reissue, OJCCD-1854-2.

Wayne Shorter

Adam's Apple. Blue Note DIDX 938. Reissue CDP 7 46403-2.

The All-Seeing Eye. Blue Note BLP 4219.

Juju. Blue Note CDP 7 84173-2. Reissue CDP 7243 8 37644-2.
Night Dreamer. Blue Note (J) GXF 3054. Reissue CDP 7 84173-2.
The Soothsayer. Blue Note (J) GXF 3054. Reissue CDP 7 84443-2.
Speak No Evil. Blue Note BLP 4194. Reissue CDP 7243 4 99001-2.

Tony Williams

Lifetime. Blue Note BLP 4180.
Spring. Blue Note BLP 4216.

Index

Jeremy Yudkin is a professor of music at the College of Fine Arts and associated faculty of the Department of African American Studies, Boston University, and Visiting Professor of Music at Oxford University. His courses include jazz history, Beethoven, Bartok, and the Beatles. He has also taught in Paris and lectured in London, Moscow, and St. Petersburg. He has been awarded fellowships from the National Endowment for the Humanities, the Marion and Jasper Whiting Foundation, and the Camargo Foundation. Professor Yudkin also teaches the Summer Music Seminars at Tanglewood—an entertaining lecture series he founded over twenty years ago. His video *Inside the Orchestra* was the winner of a 2005 Telly Award. He has served as an advisor for the new *Smithsonian Collection of Classic Jazz* and is a consultant on jazz to the *Oxford English Dictionary*. This is his eighth book. His most recent publication was *The Lenox School of Jazz: A Vital Chapter in the History of American Music and Race Relations*.